Enid Blyton

SPELLBINDING
STORIES

Look out for all of these enchanting story collections

by *Enid Blyton*

Enid Blyton

SPELLBINDING STORIES

Illustrations by Mark Beech

HODDER

HODDER CHILDREN'S BOOKS

This collection first published in Great Britain in 2023
by Hodder & Stoughton

1 3 5 7 9 10 8 6 4 2

Enid Blyton® and Enid Blyton's signature are registered trade marks
of Hodder & Stoughton Limited
Text © 2023 Hodder & Stoughton Limited
Cover and interior illustrations by Mark Beech.
Illustrations © 2023 Hodder & Stoughton Limited

A CIP catalogue record for this book is available from the British Library.

ISBN 978 1 444 96927 6

Typeset by Avon DataSet Ltd, Alcester, Warwickshire

Printed and bound in Great Britain by Clays Ltd, Elcograf S.p.A.

The paper and board used in this book are made from
wood from responsible sources.

MIX
Paper | Supporting
responsible forestry
FSC® C104740

Hodder Children's Books
An imprint of Hachette Children's Group
Part of Hodder & Stoughton Limited
Carmelite House
50 Victoria Embankment
London EC4Y 0DZ

An Hachette UK Company
www.hachette.co.uk
www.hachettechildrens.co.uk

Contents

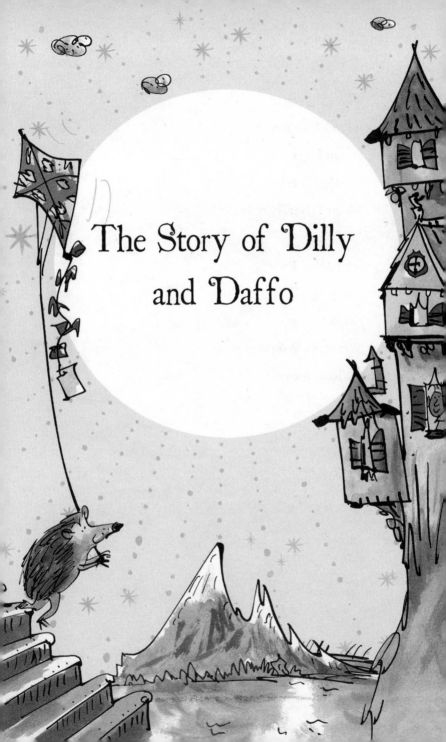

The Story of Dilly and Daffo

The Story of Dilly
and Daffo

DILLY AND Daffo were elfin twins, and they lived in Wishing Wood with old Witch Gruffles. They didn't live with her because they liked to, but because they had to. You see, she had captured them when they were babies. She had found them all alone in their buttercup cradle, and had taken them off with her to be her servants.

As they grew up she taught them to sew. She was the sort of witch who sold magic hats, cushions, sheets and curtains. She would say a spell over a cushion as it was being made, and then whoever put it beneath his head would have pleasant dreams.

Witch Gruffles was very, very bad at sewing, and very good at spells. *And*, she thought to herself, *what's the use of putting an expensive spell into a badly made cushion? I should never sell the cushion, and the spell would be wasted!*

So now you see why she taught Dilly and Daffo sewing. Elves are always clever with their fingers, and witches are usually clumsy, so Dilly and Daffo soon became very useful. In fact, as the witch rarely allowed them to do anything else but sew for her, they quickly became so clever at making all sorts of wonderful things that fairies came from far and near to buy them.

But Dilly and Daffo were very unhappy. They had no friends at all.

'Everyone seems to think we must be horrid if we live with a witch!' said Dilly.

'They think we will weave nasty spells over them, and we wouldn't,' sighed Daffo.

'Could we run away, do you think?' whispered Dilly.

4

'What would be the good?' whispered Daffo. 'We haven't any friends to run away to, and no one would help us in case Witch Gruffles came along and put a spell on them, and changed them into beetles or something.'

'Oh, dear! Well, let's be ever so nice to the fairies and elves who come to buy,' said Dilly. 'Then, perhaps, one day we will make a friend.'

But it wasn't a bit of good. All the fairies, elves, pixies and gnomes were too much afraid of old Witch Gruffles to pay any attention to the smiling elves. They just chose what they wanted, paid for it quickly and hurried away as fast as they could.

'She isn't nice,' said the fairies shudderingly. 'She ought to be sent away from Fairyland, but, as long as no one can say for certain whether she uses bad spells as well as good ones, she will have to stay.'

One day a pixie came in to buy a frilly pleasant-dream cushion. He said something that made Dilly and Daffo feel most excited.

'Thank you,' he said, as he paid Witch Gruffles for the cushion. 'Did you know that the fairy queen is passing through Wishing Wood next week? She will go through Birch Tree Glade just near here. You will see her if you watch.'

The fairy queen! Dilly and Daffo had never seen her, but they had heard all about her, and loved her. They felt most excited when they knew she was coming so near to them.

'Oh, *please* may we go and watch for her and welcome her?' they begged Witch Gruffles. 'There will be elves and fairies and pixies and gnomes cheering her as she goes, and all the trees will put on their new green leaves to welcome her. We'd like to welcome her too.'

'Well, you just *won't*,' snapped the witch, who didn't like the fairy queen at all. 'You'll stay indoors, because I shall want you to help me with a spell.'

Dilly and Daffo looked very disappointed, but they would have been more miserable still if they had guessed what the spell was the witch was going to use – for *it was a spell to capture the fairy queen.*

'And I won't let her go till she promises me half the gold in Fairyland!' chuckled the witch to herself, and began to lay her plans.

Dilly and Daffo were also making plans, for they had thought of a good idea. They had been to Birch Tree Glade to see what it was like, and had found the grass full of quaint yellow flowers, just like long trumpets. Nearby danced some windflowers with little frills of green round their necks.

The yellow flowers were talking among themselves as Dilly and Daffo came up.

'We do wish we were beautiful!' they sighed, 'but whoever saw such ugly fellows as we are! Just long, sticking-out trumpets – no pretty frills like the anemones have! We would like to be pretty and to give the queen a good welcome!'

Dilly and Daffo listened. Then they carefully looked at the quaint flowers – and the same thought struck them both.

'*We* can make you pretty!' they cried. 'We've got some yellow stuff for making cushions at home, and if you like, we'll make you each a darling little frill and sew it round your necks. Then you'll be as pretty as can be!'

They had to make the frills when Witch Gruffles wasn't looking, and they put their very tiniest stitches into them. Then the evening before the queen was expected, they ran to Birch Tree Glade and sewed the yellow frills round each flower's neck. You can't *think* how lovely they looked. They looked quite different and were so pleased that they began dancing merrily in the breeze.

'The yellow doesn't *quite* match,' said the elves, 'it's a bit paler, but never mind, you look simply *lovely*. Now we must go, as Witch Gruffles wants us to help with a spell.'

Off they went, and the flowers waited anxiously for the queen. To their great astonishment she came much sooner than they had expected – for when the moonlight was streaming down, she floated into the glade as light as thistledown.

'Welcome! Welcome!' they cried, nodding their yellow heads. 'We thought you weren't coming till the dawn! Oh, welcome, welcome!'

'Why, you perfectly lovely things!' cried the queen in delighted astonishment. 'I've never seen flowers like you before!'

Then the flowers told her about Dilly and Daffo, and how kind they had been in sewing frills on, and the queen was most interested.

'I really must go and thank them,' she said. 'Where do they live?'

The flowers told her, and off she went with her court to find the elves.

But as she got near to the witch's cottage, she heard sounds of crying and weeping coming through the night, and stopped to listen.

And then what do you think she heard? She heard Dilly's voice, and it cried, 'You wicked Witch Gruffles!

How dare you make a spell to capture our dear queen!'

And then Daffo's voice came, 'You very wicked witch! *I* won't help you in your bad spell! I love the dear fairy queen!'

'THEN I SHALL CHANGE YOU INTO BEETLES!' came the witch's voice, very angry indeed.

'We don't care!' cried the elves – and just at that moment the queen, suddenly realising what was happening, gave the signal to her court, and the Lord High Chancellor ran forward and wrenched open the door of the cottage.

And there was Witch Gruffles just going to turn the poor little elves into beetles! But in a trice she was caught and bound, and the chancellor told her if she spoke one single word *she* would be turned into a beetle.

'You are two dear little brave elves,' said the queen, 'and I've come to thank you for sewing such beautiful frills round my flowers. Your work is so lovely that I would like you to come back to the palace with me, to do all the palace sewing. Do you think you would like to?'

'Oh, Your Majesty, yes, yes, yes!' squeaked Dilly and Daffo, jumping up and down with joy; and the queen took them along with her that very same night, and very useful indeed she found them. They have lots and lots of friends now. As for old Witch Gruffles, she was sent away from Fairyland and has never been back since.

You can find the flowers that Dilly and Daffo made frills for, every springtime. They make the frills every year, and sew them on so beautifully that only if you have fairy eyes can you see the stitches. They are named after Dilly and Daffo – and, of course, you've guessed what they are – the dancing golden daffodillies that grow so brightly in your garden and mine!

Mr Very-Smart

Mr Very-Smart

THERE WAS once a little girl called Belinda whose mother was ill and very poor. Their landlord, Mr Very-Smart, came along one morning and said if they didn't pay the rent before five o'clock that afternoon, he would turn them out into the street.

Belinda didn't know *what* to do! *I'll go to the wise woman*, she thought at last. *Perhaps she can help me.*

So off she went. When the wise woman heard Belinda's story she was sorry.

'I have no money to give you,' she said. 'But see – here is a money spell. If you can work it out, you will get a sack of gold.'

Belinda took the piece of paper gladly, and hurried home. On the way she met Mr Very-Smart, and she told him about the money spell.

'A money spell!' said Mr Very-Smart greedily. 'Here, give the paper to me. *I'll* make the sack of gold come – a little girl like you couldn't work a difficult spell like this.'

'Please give my paper back to me,' begged Belinda, who knew quite well that Mr Very-Smart meant to take all the gold, if any came. But Mr Very-Smart wouldn't. He began to read the spell. This is what it said: 'Find as many white pebbles as there are petals on a wild rose; mix them with as many drops of honey as there are legs on a spider; stir as many times as there are wings on a bee; then sing the next seven magic words as fast as a blackbird sings his evening song. Then, lo and behold! A sack of gold will appear!'

Mr Very-Smart found six white pebbles; he borrowed some honey from a neighbour and put six drops of it on to the pebbles; then he stirred the mixture twice.

Now, how does a blackbird sing? he wondered, for he had never in his life listened to a bird singing. 'Oh, it's a big bird, so I expect it sings quickly.'

He chanted the seven magic words very fast indeed – and, oh my! What *do* you think happened? He was suddenly caught up by a huge wind and swept away! Belinda watched him go – and he never came back!

'He did the spell all wrong,' she said. 'He made the wrong magic come, and it's taken him away. Now *I'll* try!'

Belinda knew how many petals a wild rose had – do you? So she fetched *five* round white pebbles, not six. Then she poured *eight* drops of honey on to them, for, of course, a spider has eight legs, not six. And how many wings has a bee? Do *you* know? Belinda did, for she had used her eyes. She stirred the mixture *four* times, not twice, and then slowly and sweetly she sang the seven magic words, for she had often listened to the blackbird in the evening time, and knew exactly how he sang. He *never* hurried his song.

When she had finished there was a BANG! The pebbles and honey disappeared and in their place stood a fat sack. Belinda peeped inside – it was full of gold!

She dragged it home, and *how* delighted her mother was!

Now I wonder – could *you* have worked that spell as Belinda did?

The Pig with a Straight Tail

The Pig with a Straight Tail

THERE WAS once a pig whose tail was as straight as a poker. This worried him very much, because all the tails belonging to his brothers and sisters were very curly indeed.

'Ha!' said his little sisters. 'Look at Grunts! Whoever saw a pig with a straight tail before?'

'Ho!' said his big brothers. 'Look at Grunts! Whoever saw a pig without a kink in his tail before?'

Poor Grunts was very much upset about it.

I really must get my tail curly somehow, he thought to himself. *Now what can I do?*

He thought a little while and then he trotted

off to old Dame Criss-Cross.

'Sometimes her hair is quite straight and sometimes it is curly,' he said to himself. 'I wonder what she does to it. I will ask her.'

So he knocked on her little front door with his trotter. Dame Criss-Cross opened it, and was most surprised to see Grunts there.

'What do you want?' she asked.

'I want to know how to curl my tail,' said Grunts. 'I know you curl your hair, so I thought perhaps you could tell me.'

Dame Criss-Cross laughed till the tears came into her eyes. Then she went into her bedroom and fetched a great big curling-pin, the biggest she had got.

'Here you are, Grunts,' she said. 'Let me put your tail into this curling-pin and it will curl beautifully.'

She rolled Grunts's tail up in the pin, and, oh, dear, it did hurt! Grunts groaned loudly, but he so badly wanted a curly tail that he put up with the pain like a hero.

Off he went back to the pigsty, and, dear me, how all the big pigs and little pigs roared with laughter to see Grunts with his tail done up in a large curling-pin.

Next morning, Grunts ran off to Dame Criss-Cross again, and she undid it for him. Oh, what a fine curly tail he had! It twisted itself up like a spring, and Grunts was terribly proud of it. He stood with his back to all the other pigs whenever he could, and they admired his tail very much, for it was even curlier than theirs.

But then a dreadful thing happened. It began to rain. Grunts took no notice, for he didn't mind the rain at all; but his beautiful curly tail got wet and all the curl came out!

'Your tail's straight! Your tail's straight!' cried all the pigs, crowding round him. Grunts looked over his back, and, sure enough, his tail was as straight as a poker again.

'Oh, bother!' said Grunts in dismay. 'It's no good

putting it into curlers, that's quite plain. Now what shall I do?'

'Go to Tips the pixie and get her to put a curly spell in your tail,' said the biggest pig of all.

So off went Grunts to Tips's little cottage and banged at her door with his trotter.

'What do you want, Grunts?' she asked.

'Can you put a curly spell in my tail?' asked Grunts. 'It's so dreadfully straight.'

'Well, I'll try,' said Tips doubtfully. 'But I don't know if I've a spell that is strong enough. Your tail is really too straight!'

She fetched a blue bowl and put into it six strange things – a golden feather with a blue tip, a spider's web heavy with dew, a centre of a young daisy, the whisker of a gooseberry, a hair from a red squirrel and a spoonful of moonlight taken from a puddle. Then she stirred the mixture up together, singing a little magic song.

'Now turn round and put your tail in the bowl,'

said Tips. 'The spell will make it curly.'

So Grunts turned round and put his straight little tail into the blue bowl. The pixie stirred the mixture all over it, and gradually it became curlier and curlier. Tips was delighted.

'It has made it curly,' she said. 'But I don't know how long it will stay like that, Grunts.'

'Will rain change it?' asked the little pig.

'No,' said Tips, 'I don't think so. My, you do look fine!'

Off went Grunts back to the pigsty, and all the pigs admired him very much. But – wasn't it a pity? – the sun came out and shone down so hotly that poor Grunts's tail began to go limp again! And soon it was just as straight as ever. The sun had melted away the curly spell.

'Well, I'm sure I don't know *what* to do!' said Grunts in dismay.

'What's the matter?' asked an old witch who happened to be passing by. So Grunts told her his trouble.

'Oh, you want a very, very strong spell,' said the witch. 'You had better come to me – I can give you one that will make your tail very curly indeed.'

Now, the wicked old witch didn't mean to do anything of the sort. She just wanted to get hold of Grunts and make him into bacon. But Grunts didn't know she was wicked, and he felt most excited.

'Come to me at midnight tonight,' said the witch. 'My cottage is in the middle of Hawthorn Wood.'

So that night, at just about half past eleven, Grunts set out. It was very dark, and when he got into the wood it was darker still. Grunts began to feel frightened.

Then something made him jump terribly.

'*Too-whit, too-whit!*' said a loud voice.

'*Too-whoo, too-whoo!*' said another. Grunts gave a squeal and began to run.

He didn't know it was only a pair of owls calling to one another. Then something else gave him a fright. The moon rose and looked at him through the trees.

'Ooh!' squealed the little pig. 'What is it? It's a giant's face looking at me!'

He stumbled on through the wood, quite losing his way. Suddenly he heard two voices nearby, and against the light of the moon he saw two witches.

'Have you seen a little pig?' asked one.

'No,' said the other. 'Why?'

'Oh, one was coming to me to get his tail made curly!' said the first one, with a laugh. 'Silly pig! He didn't know I was going to catch him and make him into bacon!'

Grunts crouched down in the bushes, and stayed quite still until the witches had gone away. All his bristles stood up on his back with fright, his tail curled up with fear, and he shivered like a jelly.

What an escape I've had! he thought. *Ooh, that wicked old witch. I'll go straight home as soon as it's dawn.*

So when day came he looked around him, found the right path and scampered home as fast as he could. Wasn't he glad to see the pigsty. But what a surprise he had when he got there!

'Oh, your tail is lovely and curly!' cried all his brothers and sisters. 'Did the old witch put a spell on it?'

'No,' said Grunts in surprise, looking at his curly tail in delight. 'Now whatever made it go like that? Why, I was almost frightened out of my life!'

'It was the fright that made your tail curl!' said an old pig wisely. 'That's what it was! Didn't you feel something funny about it last night?'

'Now I come to think of it, I did,' said the little pig. 'Oh, my, what a funny thing! I escaped the old witch, got a terrible fright and a curly tail! I wonder if it will last.'

Day after day Grunts looked at his tail – and so far it is still as curly as ever. He is so pleased about it, of course!

The Hey-Diddle Pie

The Hey-Diddle Pie

IN THE end cottage of Pinniky Village lived old Dame Criss-Cross. She was just like her name, the crossest old woman that anybody had ever met. The pixies, gnomes and elves tried to like her, but oh, dear me, it was very hard work!

Just beyond her cottage the common began. It was a lovely stretch of gorse bushes, heather and fine, springy grass. Bluebells grew in the dells of the common, and in the autumn blackberries ripened in thousands on the brambles.

It was a lovely place for the children of the pixies and gnomes to play. They used to go there every day and shout and laugh from morning till night.

Old Dame Criss-Cross didn't like children. She hated to hear their jolly voices, and when she heard them laugh, she frowned till her forehead was nothing but wrinkles.

'Drat those children!' she said. 'Why can't they go and play somewhere else!'

When a ball came rolling into her garden, the children didn't dare to fetch it, and there it had to stay. They were all afraid of Dame Criss-Cross, and even when little Silver-Toes fell down and made his knee bleed, they wouldn't go to her cottage to ask for help.

One day, when Dame Criss-Cross was just walking out of her garden gate to go shopping, a crowd of pixie children came tearing round the corner and bumped right into her. Dame Criss-Cross was sent spinning and sat down with a bump. Her basket went one way and her bonnet went another.

The pixies were sorry and frightened. They hadn't meant to knock the old woman over, of course.

They picked up her basket and her bonnet, and gave them to her.

'You naughty, wicked pixies!' said the old dame, shaking her stick at them. 'You did that on purpose, so you did! Well, you're not to come past my cottage any more, do you hear? If you do, I'll punish you!'

The pixies said nothing, but they ran home to their parents. The only way to get to the common was past Dame Criss-Cross's cottage – and surely they might still play among the heather and the gorse!

'Of course you shall!' cried the folk of Pinniky Village. 'Don't you take any notice of Dame Criss-Cross! We'll send her a letter that will make her shiver and shake in her shoes!'

Then Trippit, the elfin schoolmaster, wrote a letter and this is what he said:

Dear Dame Criss-Cross,
  If you scold our children, we will come and turn you out of your cottage, and you will never be allowed

to live here again. The pixies did not mean to knock
you over, and they are sorry they did. They will come
and play on the common each day as they always do,
and if you try to stop them, we shall punish you!

When Dame Criss-Cross got that letter, how she shivered and shook! She knew quite well that if she did punish the pixies or elves, their parents would complain to the queen, and she certainly *would* be turned out of Pinniky Village!

So she had to let the children run past her cottage as usual, and they played happily on the common all day. But the old dame frowned and brooded, and wondered how she could revenge herself on Pinniky Village.

At last, she put on her cloak and her bonnet, took her broomstick to ride upon – for she was half a witch – and went flying away to see her old friend, Mother Grumpy. She told her all her troubles, and Mother Grumpy listened.

'Ah!' said her friend. 'So you want my help, do you? Well, Dame, I've a Hey-Diddle spell here that will do just what you want! It will spirit all those pixie children away, and they will never be heard of again. And no one will know you've had anything to do with it!'

'Give it to me!' begged Dame Criss-Cross eagerly.

'You must let me have ten gold pieces,' said Mother Grumpy. 'It is not a cheap spell.'

Dame Criss-Cross sighed and opened her bag. Ten gold pieces were all she had in the world – but she gave them to Mother Grumpy.

'Where is this Hey-Diddle spell?' she asked. Mother Grumpy went to a cupboard and took down a bottle full of green powder.

'Here it is,' she said. 'Whoever tastes this will at once start walking to the east, and won't stop until they come to the palace of the magician Hey-Diddle. Then they will walk into the gates and straight away become the servant of the magician.'

'What a powerful spell!' said the old dame, a little frightened. 'Where did you get it from?'

'Hey-Diddle gave it to me himself,' said Mother Grumpy. 'He often wants servants, you know, and he promised me that for every servant he got because of this green powder, he would give me a bag of gold.'

'Well, you ought to give it to me for nothing then!' cried Dame Criss-Cross. 'You will get heaps of gold because I shall make dozens of children go walking off to his palace to be his servants.'

'No, you must pay me,' said Mother Grumpy. 'But I will share the bags of gold with you, Dame. That is quite fair. But I want ten pounds now to buy a new fly-away broomstick.'

Dame Criss-Cross took the Hey-Diddle spell and flew back home on her broomstick. She was very much pleased with her morning's work. Now the next thing to do was to plan how to use the spell.

It was blackberry time just then, and the Dame saw the pixies and elves passing her cottage every day with purple-stained mouths and hands. When she thought of this she clapped her hands in delight.

'I will use the Hey-Diddle spell on a blackberry bush!' she cried. 'That's the thing to do! And I'll do it this very night!'

So when it was dark, the old woman took her lantern and went to the common. She found a blackberry bush full of ripening berries, and she set her lantern down by it.

Now first I will make the berries twice as big and black, she thought, *then the children will be sure to see them and eat them. As soon as I have made the berries big, I will scatter the green powder over the bush and say the words of the Hey-Diddle spell – and when the pixies eat them, their legs will at once march them to the east till they come to Hey-Diddle's palace! Then they will be his servants and nobody will ever know what has become of them! Ha! That will be the end of those nasty, noisy children!*

Dame Criss-Cross danced round the blackberry bush and chanted a magic song. At once all the berries on the bush grew twice as big and became very black and juicy. Then the old woman said the words of the Hey-Diddle spell and shook the bottle of green powder all over the bush, till every blackberry had a speck on it.

When the bottle was empty, Dame Criss-Cross put it into her pocket, took up her lantern and went home very pleased indeed.

The next morning, she stood at her window to watch the pixie and elfin children run past. It was a fine day and every single child ran to play on the common.

'Let's pick blackberries, let's pick blackberries!' one cried to another, and the old woman rubbed her hands gleefully.

There were many berries ripe that sunny day and the pixies and elves feasted on them – and suddenly they came to the bush over which Dame Criss-Cross had shaken the Hey-Diddle spell.

'Ooh!' cried a pixie. 'Look! Did ever you see such a wonderful crop of blackberries! Why, they are twice as big as any others! Let's pick them and eat them.'

'Wait a minute,' cried a tall elf, running up. 'No, don't let's eat them. My mother has promised to make a pie for the poor old Balloon Man, who is ill – and she asked me to choose the finest I could see. Let's pick them for the old Balloon Man, shall we?'

'Yes, yes!' cried the kind-hearted little creatures. 'We won't eat a single one! They shall be made into a wonderful pie for the old Balloon Man!'

So every one of the big blackberries was carefully picked and put into a basket. Then the pixies and elves thought it must be dinnertime, and off they ran back to Pinniky Village.

Dame Criss-Cross saw them running past her house, and she was full of surprise and very cross, for she had hoped that not one child would pass that way again – she thought that maybe all of them would be walking eastwards toward Hey-Diddle's palace.

They can't have found the bush yet, she thought. *I'll just go and see.*

So off she went – but when she saw that every berry was gone from it, she stood still in amazement.

'Oh!' she cried. 'That wicked Mother Grumpy sold me a spell that was no good! I'll go and see her tonight, and get back my ten gold pieces.'

And now, what was happening to the blackberries? Why, the tall elf had given them to his mother, and she was already very busy making a pie for the old Balloon Man. When it was finished, she sent the elf to his house.

'Here's a pie for you, Balloon Man!' cried the elf, and handed it in through the window. The Balloon Man was in bed, half asleep. He opened his eyes and nodded, and then fell fast asleep again, without really seeing what the elf had put on the window ledge. When he woke up, he saw the pie there and was astonished.

'But dear me,' he said, 'what a pity! The doctor says I mustn't eat pies or tarts this week, so I can't have it. I don't like to send it back to where it came from, for they might be hurt. What shall I do with it?'

He thought for a moment, and then he heard a knock at his door. It was little Tiptap, who was servant to Clippit the Bee-Woman, just down the road. Tiptap had brought some oranges for the Balloon Man.

'Thank you kindly,' said he. 'Oh, Tiptap – you might take this pie to Clippit. I mustn't eat pies yet, and it would be a pity to waste it.'

So Tiptap ran with the pie to her mistress – but Clippit was quite dismayed to see it.

'Goodness me, Tiptap!' she said. 'I've just done all my baking, and I have got four pies cooking in the oven now. I really can't do with another! Whatever shall we do with it?'

'What about Mother Shoo-Away and all her children?' asked Tiptap. 'I'm sure she would be pleased with it.'

'Of course she would!' said Clippit, pleased. 'Run along and take it for me, Tiptap.'

So Tiptap carried the pie to Mother Shoo-Away's

cottage. It was almost opposite Dame Criss-Cross's little house, and kind old Mother Shoo-Away had often tried to do a good turn to the cross old dame.

'Please,' said Tiptap, 'here's a pie for you from the Bee-Woman.'

'Oh, thank you!' cried Mother Shoo-Away in delight. 'That will be a great treat for my children.'

'Ooh!' cried the children, when they saw the big pie. 'Ooh! Mother, let's eat it now, shall we?'

'Well, we'll take it out into the garden and eat it there,' said Mother Shoo-Away. 'It's such a lovely day, and the kitchen is so stuffy.'

So out they all trooped into the garden, carrying their plates and spoons. Just as Mother Shoo-Away dug her knife into the pie, she caught sight of Dame Criss-Cross standing at her garden gate over the way, and Shoo-Away's kind heart made her think that it would be nice to send her a piece of the lovely pie.

'Pinkity,' she said to her eldest boy. 'Fetch the best plate and the silver spoon from the kitchen. I will send a piece of this pie to poor old Dame Criss-Cross. I'm sure the old woman looks half starved.'

Pinkity fetched the best plate and the silver spoon. Mother Shoo-Away cut a huge slice of the Hey-Diddle pie and put it on to the plate. The crust was lovely, and the big blackberries made a purple juice over the plate.

'Now run across and give it to Dame Criss-Cross,' said Shoo-Away to Pinkity. So the pixie went across the road, carrying the plate carefully.

'Please, Dame Criss-Cross,' he said politely, 'Mother sends you a slice of our pie, and hopes you will like it.'

Now Dame Criss-Cross was very hungry, for she had no money left to buy food for herself that day, as she had given it all to Mother Grumpy for the Hey-Diddle spell. So she was glad to see the slice of pie, and for once in a way gave quite a polite message of thanks. Then she started to eat it very hungrily.

Oh, what a good pie it was! What a wonderful taste

it had! Dame Criss-Cross was glad Shoo-away had sent her such a big slice.

Mother Shoo-Away was pleased that Dame Criss-Cross had taken the slice of pie. She cut up the rest of the pie, and put it on her children's plates.

'Nobody must begin until you're all served, and we can say grace for such a lovely meal,' said Shoo-Away to the children. So they all waited patiently. But just as the last child was given his plate of pie, a strange thing happened.

From across the road came a cry of dismay. Mother Shoo-Away and the children looked up. They saw Dame Criss-Cross holding on to her gate as hard as she could, while her legs seemed to be trying to walk away!

'What's the matter, what's the matter?' cried Shoo-Away and the children. They put down their plates of pie and ran to help Dame Criss-Cross.

'It's that horrid pie!' cried the old woman in a rage. 'Those Hey-Diddle blackberries have been made

44

into a Hey-Diddle pie – and I've eaten it, I've eaten it! Oh, what shall I do! I'll have to walk to the magician Hey-Diddle's palace now, and be his servant! My legs are taking me! Oh! Oh!'

She had to let go of her hold on the gate, and before Mother Shoo-away could stop her the old dame had walked quickly down the lane towards the east, and was soon out of sight.

'Well!' said Mother Shoo-Away, who knew perfectly well what a Hey-Diddle spell was, and guessed what mischief the old woman had been up to. 'Well! The wicked old dame! She must have bewitched a bush of blackberries, hoping to send all the children who ate them away to the magician Hey-Diddle. But the children must have taken them home for a pie – and somehow it came round to us.'

'And we gave a slice to Dame Criss-Cross, and she's the only one who ate it!' cried the children. 'So she's been caught by her own spell!'

'What a lucky escape for us!' said Shoo-Away. 'And

oh, how much nicer Pinniky Village will be without Dame Criss-Cross! Let us come and throw away our pie slices, for we certainly mustn't eat any now.'

So the pie was thrown away on the rubbish heap, and that night an army of rats found it and ate it up, every bit. Then off they went to Hey-Diddle's palace, for the spell was just as strong for them as for anyone else. And how cross the magician was to find rats walking into his bedroom in the middle of the night!

As for Dame Criss-Cross, nobody was ever bothered with *her* again! She had to work from morning to night for the magician, and how he laughed when he heard she had fallen into her own trap! Mother Grumpy was pleased too, because when Hey-Diddle sent her a bag of gold, she didn't have to share it with anyone.

And the only person who was miserable was Dame Criss-Cross herself – but she deserved all she got, didn't she?

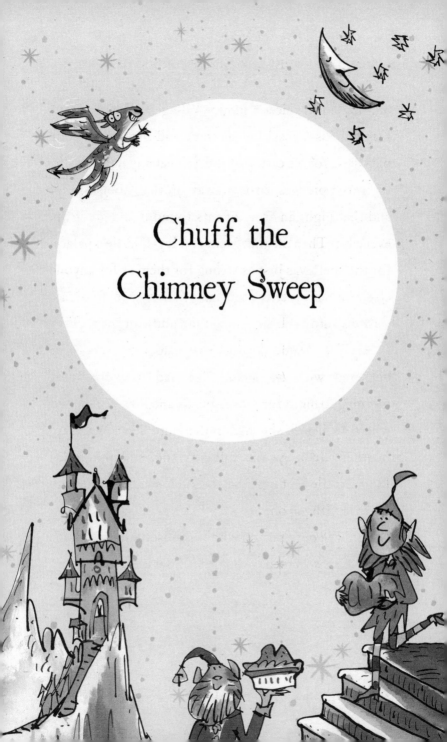

Chuff the
Chimney Sweep

Chuff the
Chimney Sweep

ONE DAY, right in the middle of the summer, Dick and Janet were walking down the lane that led to the duck pond. When they came to the big oak tree that stands in the middle of the hedge, they saw a motorcar.

But what a strange one! It was very small, smaller even than a baby motorcar, and it was painted bright red, green and yellow. The steering wheel was yellow, the seats were blue. It really was the brightest little car they had ever seen, and *so* small.

'Why, it's really not much bigger than my toy motorcar at home,' said Dick. 'The one we can both just squeeze into! I wonder who this car belongs to?'

'Let's sit in it for a minute,' said Janet. 'It does look so nice. There isn't anyone about, and we'll hop out if we see anyone coming. It would be such fun to pretend it's ours, for a minute or two!'

Now that was naughty of Janet, because she knew perfectly well that she oughtn't to get into other people's cars – but this one looked so lovely and was so bright and colourful that she felt she really must.

So Dick got in at the back, and Janet got in at the front, sitting behind the steering wheel. She took hold of it, pretending to steer – and just at that very moment there came a great noise of shouting behind the hedge, and a gnome came rushing towards them, carrying over his shoulder a pile of poles and brushes.

After him raced a most unpleasant and dirty-looking elf whose beard nearly reached the ground. He was shouting very angrily.

'You wait till I catch you, Chuff the chimney sweep!

You wait till I catch you!'

Chuff the gnome tore up to the car, and the astonished children had no time to jump out. The strange little sweep leapt into the car, pushed Janet to one side, took the steering wheel himself and started up the engine.

'*R-r-r-r-r-r!*' went the car, and leapt forward down the lane. The angry elf tripped over his beard just as he reached the car and fell flat on his nose. When he picked himself up the car was gone.

The two children were scared. Whatever was happening? And where were they going? The gnome drove at top speed, and the duck pond down the lane was passed in a flash. Then up the hill tore the car and down the other side.

'W-w-where are we going?' stammered Janet at last. 'You're taking us right away from our lane.'

The gnome didn't answer. He looked round to see if the angry elf was still following, and then made the car go even faster, so that Dick and Janet had to hold on tight, or they would have been shaken out.

'Hie!' shouted Dick at last, when they had gone quite five miles. 'Hie, Chuff the chimney sweep, stop and let us get out.'

Still the gnome took not the slightest notice. He merely hooted loudly at a cow that suddenly walked into the middle of the road. The cow didn't move. The car sped straight towards it. There was no room to pass on either side. The car must either stop or bump into the cow.

Janet and Dick clutched the sides of the car and held their breath. Surely there would be an accident? A car as tiny as Chuff's would break to pieces if it hit a great cow!

Then, to the children's enormous surprise, just as the car was about to hit the cow bang in the middle, Chuff pulled a handle near to Janet, and, hey presto! The car rose high in the air, jumped right over the cow, and landed again with a slight bump on the other side!

'Ooh!' said Dick and Janet, going quite pale. 'What a strange car!'

The cow stared at the surprising car and mooed loudly – but in a moment or two it was right away out of sight, and Chuff, Dick and Janet were over the next hill.

The children knew quite well by now that the car was a magic one, and they felt afraid of the strange little chimney sweep, who drove so fast, jumped over cows and said never a word. Janet began to wonder however they would get home again, and at last she touched Chuff's arm.

'*Please!*' she said. '*Please!* Do stop for a moment and let us get out.'

Chuff waved his hand in front of him.

'Wait till we get to the blue signpost,' he said. 'Then we shall be safe.'

Dick and Janet wondered what he meant. They looked out for the blue signpost, and at last they saw it. Just before they got there something seemed to happen to the car. It slowed down, and began to make a curious grunting noise. The gnome pressed knobs here, and pulled handles there, turning very pale as he did so.

'Get out and push, quick!' he suddenly cried to the two children. 'Quick! There's no time to be lost! If our car stops here, that elf will have us in his power! Push hard to the blue signpost, then we shall be safe!'

Dick and Janet jumped out at once. The car had almost stopped, but not quite. The children ran to the back and began to push. How they pushed! Their faces turned as red as beetroots, because they made themselves so hot. But the car went on moving, and soon it went a little faster.

'Nearly there, nearly there!' cried the gnome. 'Go on, go on, we shall be safe in a minute!'

So the children went on pushing, and at last, with a sigh of relief, they found themselves just opposite the blue signpost. The gnome jammed on his brakes and jumped out.

'Phew!' he said, and took out a big yellow handkerchief and mopped his head. 'That *was* a near squeak! Another minute and the car would have turned round and gone straight back to that horrid elf.'

'But why?' asked Dick in surprise. 'And what made him so angry?'

The gnome laughed till the tears came into his eyes.

'Well, now I'm safe, I don't mind having a good laugh,' he said, wiping his eyes. 'I'll tell you all about it. I'm Chuff the chimney sweep, and I go about sweeping chimneys all over the place. Well, Longbeard the elf wrote and asked me to sweep his, so I went to his cottage this morning. He lives in that big oak tree, you know.'

'Oh, *does* he!' said Janet in surprise. 'I didn't know anyone lived there.'

'Well, Longbeard does,' said Chuff. 'I went to him, and I swept two chimneys for him as well as ever I could, and put the soot in a big sack. The chimneys were *terribly* dirty, for they hadn't been swept for years. So I asked Longbeard to pay me sixpence a chimney, which is twice my usual price – but they were really so very dirty, and took me twice as long to do.'

'And wouldn't he pay you?' asked Dick.

'No, he wouldn't,' said Chuff, frowning. 'But I paid him out – ha, ha! Ho, ho! I emptied the bag of soot over his head! Ho, ho, ho!'

'So that's why he looked so dirty,' said Janet. 'Goodness, no wonder he was cross.'

'What I didn't remember was that Longbeard owns all the country right up to this blue signpost,' said Chuff. 'Of course, he wanted to punish me, but I ran to my car and jumped in – and no sooner was I in it, than I knew that Longbeard would send a spell after me to bring the car back to him – and then he would turn me into a frog.'

'So that's why you went so quickly,' said Dick.

'Of course,' said the gnome. 'I had to go faster than

the spell, you see. I knew that as soon as I got to the blue signpost, I was safe. But the spell nearly got us. If you hadn't got out and pushed, the car would suddenly have swung round and taken us back to Longbeard. Didn't you feel anything of the spell, children, when you were out of the car, pushing it?'

'Yes,' said Dick. 'I felt as if something was trying to drag my legs backwards.'

'Ha, that was it!' said the gnome. 'Well, we're safe now. Thank goodness we got away!'

'But how are we going to get back home?' asked Dick. 'We are miles away.'

'Now I come to think of it, what were you doing in my car?' asked the gnome, looking at them with a frown.

The children went red.

'We thought it was such a dear little car that really we *had* to sit in it for a minute,' said Dick. 'We didn't know that you were going to come running out in such a hurry.'

'Well, I can't possibly take you back yet,' said Chuff. 'I've got another chimney to sweep at a quarter to twelve, and two more at half past. What will you do? Will you come with me, and perhaps I can take you home afterwards – or would you rather stay here and try to get a lift back?'

'I think we'd rather come with you,' said Janet. 'There doesn't seem to be anybody about at all, and if we tried to walk back, I know we should get lost.'

'Come on then,' said Chuff, getting into the car again. 'It's time I was starting off to old Wizard High-in-the-Air's!'

They all of them sat in the car again and Chuff started off. For some time they ran along country roads, occasionally passing carriages and cars full of pixies and fairies who stared in the greatest astonishment at the two children.

Then suddenly Janet gave a loud cry of surprise, and pointed up in the air.

'Look, Dick, look!' she cried. 'There's a castle

on that cloud up there in the sky! Did you ever see such a strange thing?'

Dick looked – and how astonished he was! Far up in the sky was a big purple cloud, and built on it was a stone castle.

'That's where Wizard High-in-the-Air lives,' said Chuff. 'Now look out! Hold tight!'

The little chimney sweep suddenly pressed the same handle as he had used when jumping over the cow, and to the children's surprise the tiny car rose straight up in the air and went towards the castle on the cloud.

'How does it do it?' asked Dick, when he had got his breath.

'Oh, by magic,' said the gnome. 'Quite easy when you know how.'

It wasn't long before the car reached the cloud, and the gnome turned the handle back again. The car ran on to a narrow road, and went towards the castle. Dick and Janet leant out to look at the roadway. It was deep purple, and very misty, so that they were puzzled to know how the car could run on it.

'Now you'd better not get out of the car at all,' said Chuff, as he stopped before the door of the castle. 'You don't know how to walk on this cloudy stuff, and you might fall right through it and find yourselves bump on the ground far below! Be good children and stay here. I don't think the wizard will see you, and I hope he won't. He's not a very pleasant person.'

Chuff took his poles and brushes and vanished into the castle. Presently the children saw a brush come out of one of the chimneys, and they knew that Chuff was hard at work.

Suddenly they heard a voice nearby and saw a curious person looking at them.

'It must be the wizard himself,' whispered Janet. 'See what a high hat he wears.'

'Pray come and drink a cup of milk with me,' said the wizard, bowing low.

But Dick and Janet remembered what the gnome had said.

'No, thank you,' they said politely. 'We are afraid of falling through this purple cloud.'

'I will see that you don't,' said the wizard. But Dick and Janet wouldn't stir from the car. Then High-in-the-Air became angry with them, and began to mutter a string of strange words. To the children's horror, they found that their legs were beginning to move all by themselves, and against their will they were stepping out of the car!

'Chuff! Chuff! Come quickly!' cried Dick in a panic, fearful of treading on the misty roadway. He held on to the car, while one of his legs stepped down to the road. Goodness, it sank deep into the purple road, and Dick knew he would fall right through it.

'Chuff! Chuff!' he called again.

To his great joy he suddenly saw the little chimney sweep racing down the castle steps, a sack over one shoulder and his brushes over the other.

When he saw what the wizard was doing, he ran straight at him, pushed him over with a brush and then emptied the soot over his head. Then he leapt into the car, started it up and drove straight off the cloud down to earth again.

'Well, that's the second person I've emptied soot over today,' said Chuff. 'I shall be making a lot of enemies, there's no doubt of that. So that nasty old wizard was trying to make you go into his castle, was he?'

'Yes,' said Dick, 'and I was so afraid of falling through the cloud. My leg went right through it.'

'So did mine,' said Janet. 'Oh, I *am* so glad you came when you did, Chuff!'

'Yes, but I've not been paid for the chimney I swept,' said the gnome dolefully. 'Never mind. The next place I go to is very nice. It's old Mother Hubbard's. Have you heard of her?'

'Not the one whose cupboard was bare, and she

couldn't give her poor dog a bone?' said Dick in surprise.

'The very same,' said Chuff. 'But she's come into some money since then, you know, and so now her cupboard is always full. She has twenty-four dogs, and feeds them all well. She lives in a little cottage on the top of the hill. It's painted yellow, so look out for it.'

They soon saw it, and in about fifteen minutes they pulled up in front of the yellow door. Mother Hubbard came out and welcomed them.

'Why, who are your two friends?' she cried in surprise, when she saw the children.

'This is Dick, and this is Janet,' said Chuff. They all shook hands politely, and Mother Hubbard told the children to sit down on a seat in her little garden.

'You can go and sweep the two chimneys now,' said the old woman to Chuff. 'And when you've finished, go and wash in the bathroom, and then we'll all sit down to a nice glass of lemonade and some chocolate buns hot out of the oven!'

Chuff went off to do his work, and the children looked at Mother Hubbard.

'Have you still got that cupboard?' asked Janet.

'Bless you, yes!' said Mother Hubbard, beaming. 'Do you mean to say you know about that?'

'Oh, yes,' said Dick, and he recited the rhyme about Mother Hubbard and the bare cupboard. She was very much delighted, and took them indoors to see the very cupboard. But when she swung the door open, what a sight met their eyes!

The cupboard was full to bursting with good things! There were cakes and puddings, tarts and buns. There were big plates of bones on one shelf, and a tin of biscuits on another.

'Those are for my twenty-four dogs,' said Mother Hubbard. 'You see, my cupboard isn't bare now, is it?'

'Oh, no,' said Dick. 'Could we see the dogs, do you think? And have you still got that one who wanted a bone and couldn't have it, because your cupboard was bare?'

'Yes,' said the old lady. 'Come and see him.'

She led them to a yard, and there were the twenty-four dogs, as clean as new pins, and all wagging their tails like clockwork. The old dame called one dog to her, a little spotted one.

'This is the dear old dog who lived with me when I was so poor,' she said.

She let him out of the yard, and he trotted back with them to the garden. By that time Chuff had finished the chimneys, and they could hear him whistling in the bathroom as he washed himself clean.

'He's nearly ready,' said Mother Hubbard. 'I'll go and get the lemonade. Stay here for a minute with the dog.'

The children played with the dog till Mother Hubbard came back carrying a tray with four glasses of lemonade on it, and a dish of lovely chocolate buns. There was a bone too, and that was for the dog, who at once sat up and begged for it.

Then Chuff came running out, looking very clean, and they all sat down to the lemonade and cakes. How the children did enjoy them – they were quite the nicest buns they had ever tasted, and as for the lemonade, it was delicious.

'Mother Hubbard, what am I to do with these children?' asked Chuff, when they had all finished. 'I daren't take them back home in my car, because I'm afraid of meeting Longbeard the elf again, and I emptied soot over him this morning, so I'm afraid he won't be pleased with me.'

'Well, there's a bus running to Blackberry Hill in a moment or two,' said the old lady. 'Isn't that near where they live?'

'Yes, that's the hill just behind the duck pond!' said Dick in surprise. 'But I didn't know buses went there! I didn't even know there was a road there! There were only tiny rabbit paths when Janet and I picked blackberries there last summer.'

'Oh, you wouldn't *see* our buses!' said Chuff, laughing. 'They are invisible to your eyes when you are out of our land. But hurry up, there's no time to lose. I can hear the bus coming now!'

The children thanked Mother Hubbard and said goodbye. Then they ran off with Chuff to where a small blue bus stood on the hillside. They scrambled on and waved goodbye to the little chimney sweep.

'*R-r-r-r-r!*' The bus started off, and soon Mother Hubbard's cottage was lost in the distance. The people in the bus stared at the children, and Dick and Janet stared back too, for the passengers were really very strange.

There was a rabbit, a fox, two pixies, a gnome and three fairies. They all carried basket, and had been marketing, for their baskets were full. The conductor was a mole, and he gave them two tickets for a penny when they said Blackberry Hill.

It really wasn't very long before they saw that the bus was going up a rabbit path on Blackberry Hill, and they were astonished to be there so quickly. They jumped out, and were just going to shout goodbye to the other passengers, when to their great amazement they found that the bus had vanished completely, although they could still hear its engine running!

'That's just what the chimney sweep said,' said Janet. 'Do you remember, Dick? He said that we couldn't see the pixie buses in *our* land, even though they were there!'

'So he did,' said Dick. 'Well, come on, Janet, let's race home and tell Mother all we've done this morning.'

But Mother really *couldn't* believe them! She said it was all too astonishing.

'Well, Mother, you must come and see elf Longbeard in his oak tree,' said Janet at last. So they all went next day to the big oak tree in the lane.

But they couldn't find anyone there at all! The tree was hollow, but inside it was quite empty. Janet was *so* disappointed – and then suddenly she spied something on the floor of the tree. It was soot!

'There!' she cried. 'That shows you, Mother! Longbeard *was* living here, even if he's gone now! Look at the soot on the floor!'

So Mother *had* to believe their wonderful story – and the two children are always looking out for Chuff the chimney sweep, to take him home to tea. But they have never seen him again; isn't it a pity?

The Enchanted Egg

The Enchanted Egg

NOW ONCE upon a time Sly-One the gnome did a marvellous piece of magic that nobody had ever done before.

He stirred together in a golden bowl, lit by moonlight, many peculiar things. One of them was the breath of a bat, another was a snippet of lightning, and yet another was an echo he had got from a deep cave.

He didn't quite know what would come of all these strange things and the dozens of others he had mixed together – but he guessed it would be something very powerful indeed.

Whatever it is, it will bring me greatness and power,

thought Sly-One, stirring hard. *I shall be able to do what I like.*

Sly-One was not a nice person. Nobody liked him, though most people were afraid of him because he was very cunning. But he did not use his brains for good things, only for bad ones.

He stirred away for two whole hours, and soon the curious mixture in the golden bowl began to turn a colour that Sly-One had never in his life seen before. Then it began to boil! As it boiled, it twittered!

'Very strange indeed,' said Sly-One to himself, half scared. 'A very curious twitter indeed. It sounds like the twitter of the magic hoolloopolony bird, which hasn't been seen for five hundred years. Surely this magic mixture of mine isn't going to make a hoolloopolony bird! How I wish it was, because if I had that bird I could do anything I liked. It is so magic that it has the power to obey every order I give it. Why, I could be king of the whole world in a day!'

But the mixture didn't make a bird. It twittered for

a little while longer, turned another curious colour and then boiled away to nothing.

Or almost nothing. When Sly-One, disappointed, looked into the bowl, he saw something small lying at the bottom of it. It was a tiny yellow egg with a red spot at each end.

Sly-One got very excited indeed when he saw it. 'It's not a hoolloopolony bird – but it's the egg! My word, it's a hoolloopolony's egg! Now, if only I can get it hatched, I shall have one of those enchanted birds for my very own – a servant that can obey any order I think of making!'

He picked up the egg very gently. It hummed in his fingers and he put it back into the bowl. How was he to get it hatched?

I'd better find a bird's nest and put it there, thought Sly-One. *A really fine nest, safe and warm and cosy, where this enchanted egg can rest and be hatched out. I must go round and inspect all the nests there are. I shall soon find a good one.*'

He left the egg in the bowl and covered it with a silver sheet. Then he put on his boots and went out. It was the nesting season for birds, and Sly-One knew there would be plenty of nests to choose from.

He soon found one. It was a robin's, built in a ditch. Sly-One walked up to inspect it, and knelt down beside it.

'It's made of moss and dead leaves and bits of grass,' he said. 'It's well-hidden because there are plenty of dead leaves lying all round. Perhaps this will do.'

But just then a dog came sniffing into the ditch and Sly-One changed his mind. 'No, no! It's not a good place for a nest, if dogs can tramp about near it. Why, that dog might easily put his paw on the enchanted egg and smash it if I put it here!'

So he went off to find another nest. He saw some big ones high up in a tree and he went up to look at them. They were rooks' nests, big and roomy.

They look safe enough, high up here, thought Sly-One.

Made of good strong twigs too. No dog could tread on these high nests!

He sat down in one to see what it was like. Just then a big wind blew and the tree rocked the nest violently. Sly-One was frightened. He climbed out quickly.

'Good gracious!' he said to the rooks. 'I wonder why you build your nests quite so high in the trees. The wind will blow your nests to and fro and out will come your eggs!'

'Caw!' said a big rook scornfully. 'Don't you know that when a stormy summer is expected we build lower down and when a calm one comes, we build high up? We always know! No wind will blow our nests down. Why do you come to visit them, Sly-One? You don't lay eggs!'

Sly-One didn't answer. He slid down the tree and came to a hole in the trunk. He put his head in and saw a heap of sawdust at the bottom. It was a little owl's nest. Sly-One felt about, and didn't like it.

Not at all comfortable for an enchanted egg, he thought.

A good idea though for a nest, deep down in a tree hole. Very, very safe!

'If you want another kind of hole, ask the kingfisher to show you his,' hissed the little owl. 'Do you want to hide from your enemies or something, Sly-One? Then the kingfisher's nest is just the place!'

So Sly-One went to the brilliant kingfisher who sat on a low branch over the river and watched for fish. 'Where is your nest?' asked Sly-One.

'Down there, in that hole in the bank,' said the kingfisher, pointing with his big, strong beak. 'Right at the end. You'll see it easily.'

Sly-One found the hole and crawled into it. At the end was a peculiar nest, made of old fish bones arranged together. It smelt horrible.

'I feel sick!' said Sly-One, and crawled out quickly. 'Fancy making a nest of smelly old fish bones! Certainly I shan't put my precious enchanted egg there!'

He saw the house martins flying in the air above him and he called to them. 'Where are your nests?

I want to find a nice, cosy, safe one to put something precious in.'

'See that house?' said a house martin, flying close to him. 'See the eaves there? Well, just underneath we have built our nests. They are made of mud, Sly-One.'

'What!' said Sly-One, looking up at the curious mud-nests in amazement. 'Are those your nests – those peculiar things made of mud, stuck against the walls of the house? They might fall down at any minute! And fancy living in a mud-nest! No, that won't do, thank you.'

'Coo-ooo,' said a woodpigeon, flying near. 'Would my nest do for you, Sly-One? I don't know what you want it for – but I have a very nice nest indeed.'

'What's it made of?' asked Sly-One.

'Oh – just two sticks and a little bit of moss!' said the woodpigeon, and showed Sly-One the tree in which she had built her nest.

'Why, you can see right through it, it's so flimsy!' said Sly-One in horror, thinking that his enchanted egg would certainly fall through the pigeon's nest and land on the ground below.

Then he went to the lark, but the lark said that she just laid her eggs in a dent in the ground. She showed him her eggs, laid in a horse's hoofmark in a field.

'Ridiculous!' said Sly-One. 'Why, anyone might run over those eggs and smash them. A most silly place for a nest. I want somewhere that nobody could possibly tread on.'

'Well,' said the lark, offended, 'why not go up to the steep cliffs then, where some of the seabirds lay their eggs. Look, do you see the great bird there? He's a guillemot. Call him down and ask him to carry you to where he puts his eggs. They are up on the steep cliffs, where nobody can even climb.'

Soon Sly-One was being carried on the guillemot's strong wings to the high cliff. There, on a ledge, was a big egg, laid by the guillemot.

'Do you mean to say you just put it there on this ledge?' said Sly-One. 'It might fall off at any moment, when the wind blows strongly.'

'Oh, no it won't,' said the guillemot. 'Do you see its strange shape? It's made that way, narrow at one end, so that when the wind blows, it just rolls round and round in the same place. It doesn't fall off.'

'Oh,' said Sly-One. He thought of his enchanted egg. No, that wasn't the right shape to roll round and round. It would certainly roll right off the cliff if the wind blew. It wouldn't be any good putting it there and asking the guillemot to hatch it for him.

He went to see a few nests made of seaweed that other seabirds showed him. But they smelt too strong and he didn't like them. He went back to the wood near his home, wondering and wondering what nest would be best for his precious egg.

He saw a long-tailed tit go to her nest in a bush. He parted the branches and looked at it. It was a most extraordinary ball-shaped little nest, made of hundreds and hundreds of soft feathers! Perhaps it would be just right for the hoolloopolony egg.

'There's no room for another egg,' said the long-tailed tit. 'I have to bend my long tail right over my head as it is, when I sit in my ball of a nest. When my eleven eggs hatch out, there won't be any room at all!'

Then Sly-One met a big grey bird with a barred chest. The bird called, 'Cuckoo!' to him and made him jump.

'Oh, cuckoo, so you're back again,' said Sly-One. 'Where's your nest?'

'I don't make one,' said the cuckoo. 'I always choose a good, cosy, safe nest to put my eggs in, belonging to somebody else. I don't bother about building!'

'Well,' said Sly-One, 'as you're used to finding good nests for your eggs, perhaps you can help me. I want one for an enchanted egg. I want a good safe nest, with a bird who will hatch out my egg and look after the baby bird for me, till it's old enough to come to me and do magic spells.'

'Ah, I'm the one to help you then,' said the cuckoo

at once. 'I can pick up eggs in my beak easily. I've just put an egg into a wagtail's nest. Wagtails make good parents. I'll put your enchanted egg there too, if you like.'

And that's just what the cuckoo did. Sly-One fetched the little egg from the golden bowl, and the cuckoo took it in her beak and popped it into the wagtail's nest up in the ivy. She showed Sly-One her own egg there too.

Sly-One was pleased. *Now my egg will be safe*, he thought. *How clever the cuckoo is! She's used to finding good nests for her eggs. I ought to have asked her advice at first, instead of wasting my time inspecting all those other nests.*

One day Sly-One went to see how his egg was getting on, and to his surprise the cuckoo's egg had already hatched, though it had been laid after the wagtail's eggs. And also to his surprise, there was only one wagtail egg in the nest, besides his own enchanted egg. Sly-One saw the other one lying broken on the ground. He wondered what had happened.

He didn't know the habits of the baby cuckoo. That little bare, black, baby bird didn't like anything in the nest with him. He had actually pitched the wagtail's egg out of the nest! Now he was lying resting, waiting for strength to pitch the other eggs out too!

He did pitch out one egg – the other wagtail egg. He waited till the mother wagtail was off the nest for a few minutes, then he set to work. He got the wagtail egg into a little hollow on his back, climbed slowly up the side of the nest – and then over went the little egg to the ground below. Another egg gone. Now there was only the hoolloopolony egg left. The baby cuckoo sank back, exhausted.

Then the enchanted egg hatched out into a dainty little yellow bird with a red head. It lay in the nest close to the baby cuckoo. When the wagtail came back she looked at the two baby birds and loved them. She didn't know they were not really her own.

'I'll go and fetch grubs for you,' she said, and flew off.

As soon as she was gone the baby cuckoo wanted to have the nest all to himself. What was this warm bundle pressing close against him? He didn't like it. In fact he couldn't bear it!

Somehow he managed to get the tiny bird on to his back. Somehow he managed to climb up the side of the nest to the top. He gave a heave – and over the top of the nest went the baby hoolloopolony bird, right to the ground below.

It twittered there helplessly. The wagtail came back but didn't notice it. She fed the hungry baby cuckoo and thought what a wonderful child he was. She didn't seem to miss the other at all.

When Sly-One came along to see how his wonderful egg was getting on, he found only the baby cuckoo there in the nest! On the ground lay the tiny hoolloopolony bird.

Sly-One gave a cry. He picked up the tiny bird and

put it into his pocket to keep it warm. He sped to the wise woman with it, and begged her to help it.

'Sly-One,' said the wise woman. 'I know why you want this bird. When it grows, it will be able to do powerful magic for you. Well, Sly-One, you are not a nice person and I am not going to rear up a bird to work for you.'

Sly-One was very angry. 'How was I to know the bad ways of baby cuckoos?' he cried. 'The cuckoo is not a good bird. But how was I to know?'

'You are not really very clever, Sly-One,' said the wise woman softly. 'I could have told you the ways of all birds and animals, though you should know them yourself. I am glad you chose the cuckoo to help you! Now you will never own a hoolloopolony bird, and you will never be king of the world!'

He wasn't of course, and a very good thing too. As for the tiny bird, it did get better, though Sly-One didn't know. The wise woman kept it, and then set it free. It is full of magic, but no one knows that.

It's no good trying to catch it if you see it, because it can't be caught.

Whose nest would you have put the egg into? There are such a lot of different ones to choose from, aren't there?

A Pins and Needles
Spell

A Pins and Needles Spell

'WE'RE GOING to have a meeting this afternoon to decide what to give Princess Peronel for a birthday present,' said Whiskers the magical brownie, to Jinks and Cheery.

'Well, don't ask old Meanie then,' said Jinks. 'He made an awful fuss last year, and wouldn't vote even a penny towards a present.'

'And the princess is *such* a dear,' said Cheery. 'Always a smile and a wave for everyone. I vote we buy her a pair of dancing shoes, and get the pixie Fly-High to fetch a couple of tiny stars from the sky, to put on the slippers' toes. Think how her feet would twinkle when she dances!'

'Now that's a really bright idea!' said Whiskers, pleased. 'Bring it up at the meeting, Cheery. It's to be held in the Toadstool Wood, and Gobo is growing a few toadstools for us to sit on.'

'Right. I'll tell the others,' said Jinks. 'But we *won't* ask old Meanie!'

They didn't ask Meanie – but he heard of the meeting, of course, and was very angry because he hadn't been invited. He went straight to Gobo, Jinks and Cheery.

'I shall come!' he said. 'And what's more I shall talk the whole time, and tell you what nonsense it is to give presents to a rich princess, and nobody else will get a word in!'

'You did that last time,' said Gobo. 'That's why we're not asking you to the meeting. You can't come if you're not asked.'

'That's just where you're wrong!' said Meanie fiercely. 'I *shall* come. I know where you're all meeting

– in the Toadstool Wood!'

'I forbid you to come!' said Gobo sternly. 'And don't dare to disobey – or I'll put a dreadful spell on you!'

'Don't be so silly,' said Meanie. '*You* put a spell on *me*? Why, you couldn't put a spell on a beetle! What *sort* of spell, I'd like to know?'

'I might put a "Tick-Tock Spell" on you,' said Gobo. 'So that you could only tick-tock like a clock, instead of speaking. Or a Sleepy Spell, so that you fell asleep. Or a Pins and Needles Spell . . .'

'And what exactly is *that*?' said Meanie mockingly. 'I've never heard of it in my life – and neither have you, Gobo. This is all a bit of make-up! Pins and Needles Spell, indeed!'

'A Pins and Needles Spell is a spell that, quite suddenly, makes you feel as if there are pins and needles sticking hard into you!' said Gobo solemnly. 'It's very, very painful. I think I *will* put that spell on you, Meanie – and when *that* works, I'll put *another* one on you – the Tick-Tock one, that will make everyone laugh at you!'

And, to the surprise of Jinks and Cheery, Gobo suddenly clapped his hands and danced all round the surprised Meanie, singing loudly.

'Here's a Pins and Needles Spell,
Prick him hard and jab him well,
Make him howl and make him yell,
Here's a Pins and Needles SPELL!'

Meanie laughed. 'Well? Where are your pins and needles? *I* haven't felt any! Don't try and make spells, Gobo – you don't know anything about them.'

'Oh, the spell will only work if you come and spoil our meeting,' said Gobo solemnly. 'Not unless. So keep away, Meanie, unless you want suddenly to feel jabbed and pricked all over!'

Meanie went off, still laughing. 'I'll come to the meeting all right,' he shouted back. 'And I'll certainly tell you what I think about spending our money on princesses!'

'Horrid fellow!' said Cheery. 'Why, our Princess Peronel is our great friend – we've watched her grow up from a tiny baby into the merriest child in the kingdom. Gobo, you shouldn't have said that spell – you *know* it won't work! You don't know any magic, and never have. You'll only make us look foolish this afternoon, when Meanie comes to the meeting and no spell happens!'

'You wait and see,' said Gobo. 'There are more ways than one of making a spell happen. I can do spells without magic!'

'Rubbish!' said Jinks. 'Well – we'll see you at the meeting. You've got to grow fifteen toadstools – sixteen, if Meanie comes, and I'm pretty certain he will.'

That afternoon Gobo was very busy. He grew toadstool after toadstool for seats. He draped each one with a little cloth that hung to the ground, for

Gobo liked to do things well.

Then he disappeared into the ditch, and talked to someone there for a long time. Who was it? Ah, you wait and see! Anyway, the Someone came to the ring of toadstools with him, and stood there patiently while Gobo draped *him* with a little cloth too! He looked exactly like another seat.

The magical brownies began to come to the meeting in twos and threes. Gobo showed them to their seats. 'No – don't sit *there*,' he kept saying, pointing to one draped seat. 'That's for Meanie, if he comes. It's a seat with a *Pins and Needles Spell*!'

'Dear old Gobo – *you* can't make spells – you know you can't!' said Cheery. 'Now, just don't say any more about Pins and Needles, for goodness' sake.'

Soon they were all sitting down, and the draped toadstool seats each held a magical brownie. Only one seat had no one on it – and that was the empty one left for Meanie – if he came.

The meeting began – and no Meanie was there.

Cheery got up and made a splendid little speech about birthdays, and how they gave everyone a good chance to show people how much you loved them. So what kind of a present should they give Princess Peronel?

And then a loud laugh came through the trees, and Meanie strode into the toadstool ring. 'I heard your silly speech!' he cried. 'A lot of nonsense. Now just let me tell you what *I* think!'

'Sit down,' said Cheery. 'It's Jinks's turn to speak next. SIT DOWN, I SAY!'

'Here's *your* seat, Meanie,' said Gobo, and pointed to the empty one. Meanie glared round and sat down in a temper – sat down very hard indeed.

Then he suddenly gave such a loud yell that the magical brownie next to him fell right off his toadstool in fright.

'OOOOOH!' bellowed Meanie, 'the Pins and Needles Spell! OOOOH!'

And he leapt up into the air as if he had been stung

and ran wailing through the trees, clutching the back of his trousers as he went.

'Good gracious – what's the matter with *him*?' said Whiskers in surprise.

'Pins and Needles, OOOOOH!' came Meanie's voice in the distance.

'What does he mean?' said Jinks in wonder. 'Goodness me – you don't mean to say your spell *worked*, Gobo?'

'It seems to have worked very well,' said Gobo, grinning. 'Anyway – Meanie's gone – let's get on with the meeting.'

They all sat down again, and then Jinks got up to make *his* speech. 'I am happy to think that now Meanie has been sent away by Gobo's extraordinary Pins and Needles Spell, we can get on with our meeting,' he began. Then he stopped suddenly, and stared in fright at the one empty seat – the seat that had been Meanie's!

'I say – look! Meanie's seat is walking off!' cried Jinks in a panic. '*Walking!* Whoever heard of a toadstool *walking*? I'm scared! What with Pins and Needles Spells and Walking Toadstools . . .'

Gobo began to laugh. He laughed and he laughed. Then he beamed round at everyone. 'Didn't I tell you there was more than one way of making spells happen? Well, let me show you how *mine* happened!' And he began to run after the draped seat that was solemnly walking away all by itself. 'Hey, Pins and Needles, stop!'

The seat stopped. Gobo ran up to it and tore off the cloth that was round it.

And will you believe it – it was a prickly *hedgehog*!

The hedgehog promptly curled itself up into a spiky ball, and Gobo laughed. 'There you are!' he said to his friends – 'My Pins and Needles Spell . . . the hedgehog! I just got him to come here and let me drape a covering over him. Wasn't he a *wonderful* spell? I never *dreamt* that Meanie would sit down quite so hard!'

How everyone roared! Whiskers held his sides and

laughed so much that he had to lie down and roll on the grass.

'A Pins and Needles Spell – and it was only Prickles the hedgehog! Oh, to think you've got rid of that awful Meanie by playing a silly trick on him like that!'

'And Meanie *sat* on Prickles – sat down hard in a temper!' cried Cheery. 'Oh, I shall never forget this, all my life long. Gobo, you may be no good at *real* spells – but you are *wonderful* at pretend ones!'

Gobo couldn't help feeling pleased. 'Now perhaps you won't laugh at me quite so much because I know so little magic,' he said. 'Well – let's get on with the meeting!'

So there they are, deciding to buy those dancing slippers for Princess Peronel, and wondering who can get the stars to twinkle on the toes – and laughing out loud whenever they think of poor well-pricked Meanie. He'll never come back again, that's certain. He's *much* too scared of clever old Gobo!

The Magic Treacle Jug

The Magic Treacle Jug

NOW ONCE when Miggle the goblin was walking home at night through Goblin Village, he saw a light in Mother Tick-Tock's cottage window. He stopped and thought for a moment.

'I think I'll go and peep in,' he said to himself. 'Mother Tick-Tock's grandfather was a wizard, and it's said that she knows plenty of useful spells. I might see something interesting if I go and peep.' Miggle was very well known in Goblin Village for his nosy ways. He just could not resist creeping up garden paths and peeping through people's windows. 'What a cunning fellow you are!' said Miggle to himself. 'I am bound to see something exciting at Mother Tick-Tock's house.'

So he crept into the front garden and peeped in at the lit window. Mother Tick-Tock was there, cutting large slices of bread, one after the other.

I suppose those are for her children's supper, thought Miggle, counting them. *One, two, three, four, five, six, seven – yes, they are. Goodness me – does she give them just dry bread for their suppers, poor things? I thought that Mother Tick-Tock was a very kind lady. I am sure that she must feed her children more than just dry bread.*

He watched carefully. He saw Mother Tick-Tock take up a small blue jug and he heard her speak to it. 'Fancy speaking to a jug! That really is odd,' exclaimed Miggle. 'I knew I would see something unusual if I peered through this window – how right I was! I have never heard anyone speak to a jug before. Whatever next?'

He stood on his tiptoes so that he could see right into Mother Tick-Tock's kitchen. *Well, I don't want to miss anything!* thought Miggle. *This is ever so exciting.* His eyes were as big as saucers. Then he pressed his ear very close to the window so he could hear what Mother Tick-Tock was saying to the jug.

> *'Pour me treacle,*
> *strong and sweet,*
> *For a Very Special Treat!'*

And, to Miggle's surprise, the jug left Mother Tick-Tock's hand, poised itself above a slice of bread, and poured out good, thick, yellow treacle! Then it balanced itself above the next slice and poured more treacle. Then it went to the third slice.

Good gracious me! How can a little jug like that hold so much treacle! thought Miggle in surprise. *Look at it, pouring thickly over one slice after another. Mother Tick-Tock's children will be having a tasty supper this evening. What lovely treacle too! I think that must be the finest treacle that I have ever seen. Oooh, I wish I had some of it!*

Mother Tick-Tock suddenly caught sight of Miggle's face at the window, and, leaving the jug pouring treacle on the last slice of all, she ran to the window, shouting angrily. Miggle disappeared at once and ran home at top speed. He was afraid of Mother Tick-Tock. He ran as fast as he could and he soon reached his little cottage.

But he couldn't forget that wonderful Treacle Jug. To think of having sweet treacle at any time! Miggle loved treacle more than anything else in the world.

How lucky Mother Tick-Tock's children were. No wonder he so often saw them about with thick slices of bread and treacle. 'So that's why her children always look so happy,' said Miggle. 'Imagine – all that treacle!'

Now two days later Miggle made himself a fine pudding. But when he came to taste it, he found that he had left out the sugar. Oooh – how horrid it was!

Now, if only I could borrow that Treacle Jug! thought Miggle longingly. *I could have treacle all over my pudding and it would be one of the nicest I'd ever had. Treacle would make this pudding go down a treat. I wonder if Mother Tick-Tock would lend me the jug.*

Just at that very moment Miggle saw someone passing his cottage, and who should it be but Mother Tick-Tock herself, on her way to visit a friend, Mrs Know-A-Lot. Miggle knew that she went to visit Mrs Know-A-Lot every week. Mother Tick-Tock was often gone for the best part of a day as Mrs Know-A-Lot lived on the other side of town.

Miggle watched her go down the road, and a small thought uncurled itself in his mind.

Couldn't I just borrow the Treacle Jug for a few minutes? Nobody would ever know. And if it's a magic jug, the treacle would never, never come to an end, so it wouldn't matter my having just a very little! I would not need it for very long. I am sure that Mother Tick-Tock would never find out.

He sat and thought about it, looking at his sugarless pudding. He licked his lips at the thought of all that treacle. 'This pudding needs treacle!' he declared. Then he popped it back into the oven to keep warm, and ran out of the front door very quickly indeed. *I must get that jug before I change my mind!* he thought. *I'll use it to cover my pudding with treacle, then I'll take it straight back. Run, Miggle, run!*

He came to Mother Tick-Tock's cottage. The door was locked, but the window was open just a crack – a big enough crack for a small goblin to put in an arm and reach on to the shelf for a small blue jug! There! He had got it. But how strange – it was quite empty!

I'd better not go too fast with it, in case I fall and break it, he thought. *I would be in such trouble if I broke the jug!* So he put it under his coat and walked back slowly. He felt very excited indeed. He couldn't wait to get home and tuck into his delicious pudding. He patted the Treacle Jug under his coat and carried on his way.

It did not take Miggle long to reach his little cottage. He thought about treacle pudding all the way home and he was ever so careful to make sure that the jug came to no harm! He stood the blue jug on his table and fetched his pudding from the oven. 'Ha, pudding – you're going to taste very nice in a minute!' he said, and set it down in the middle of his table. He picked up the jug and spoke to it solemnly, just as Mother Tick-Tock had.

'Pour me treacle, strong and sweet, For a Very Special Treat!' said Miggle. The little jug left his hand at once and poised itself over the pudding. It tilted – and to Miggle's great delight, a stream of rich golden treacle poured out and fell on his pudding. Miggle's mouth began to water. Oooh! That pudding was going to taste very, very nice! Very nice indeed. The pudding smelt delicious. What a clever goblin he was. Surely he was the cleverest goblin in Goblin Village! 'Treacle pudding here I come!' cried Miggle gleefully.

'There! That's enough, thank you, little Treacle Jug,' said Miggle at last, smacking his lips together. His mouth started to water again when he thought about how good the pudding was going to taste. Miggle did so love treacle!

'That's perfect, I am sure it will taste delicious. Don't pour any more, or the treacle will spill out of the dish.' But the jug took no notice at all. It went on pouring steadily and Miggle saw that the treacle was now dripping over the edges of the pudding dish. 'Hey! Didn't you hear what I said!' he cried. 'Stop, jug! You'll ruin my tablecloth!'

But the jug didn't stop. It still hung there in the air, treacle pouring from its little spout. And by this time, there was a thick coat of treacle all over his table. In fact, the tablecloth was disappearing quickly beneath the steady stream of treacle.

Miggle was angry. 'Hey! I said stop!' he shouted. 'That's my best tablecloth! I'll never get that clean. I shall probably have to buy a new one!' He snatched at the jug, but it hopped away in the air and went on pouring in another place.

'Stop, jug! Don't pour treacle into my armchair!'

shouted Miggle. 'Oh my goodness, look what you've done! Emptied treacle all over the seat of my chair and the cushion! Come away from there!'

Miggle chased after the Treacle Jug. 'I command that you stop pouring treacle,' he bellowed. By now the little goblin had turned quite red in the face. He snatched at the jug again, but it wouldn't let itself be caught. It got away from his grabbing hand just in time and hung itself up in the air just above the washtub, which was full of Miggle's dirty clothes, soaking in the suds there.

'Hey!' cried Miggle in alarm. 'Not over my washing, for goodness' sake! Stop, I say! Don't you see what you're doing? You're not supposed to pour treacle over chairs and washtubs, only over puddings and tarts. Oh, you mischievous jug! Wait till I get you! I'll break you in half!'

By this time poor Miggle was quite out of breath from chasing the jug around the room. 'Oh, please will you stop!' he pleaded. 'Look at the mess you have made. It will take me hours to clean the house. Come here!' He snatched at the jug again, but it swung away in the air and this time hung itself over the nice new hearth rug.

'Don't you realise treacle is only supposed to be poured over food?' yelled Miggle. 'It is not supposed to be poured over tables and chairs. And it is definitely not to be poured over my brand new hearth rug!' But it was too late!

Trickle, trickle, trickle – the rich, sticky treacle poured down steadily over the rug, and poor Miggle tried to pull it away. But he soon found himself standing in treacle, for it spread gradually over the floor.

'Oooh, my poor hearth rug!' moaned Miggle. 'My poor new hearth rug. I shall have to buy a new rug and a new tablecloth now.' Poor Miggle shook his head in despair. 'Even my shoes are covered in treacle. How I wish I had not taken the jug from Mother Tick-Tock's house! It is all my fault for being so greedy. Everybody is always telling me I will get into trouble one day for being so nosy – and they were right!'

Then Miggle began to feel very alarmed indeed. What was he to do with this mad Treacle Jug? He simply *must* stop it somehow.

Ah – I've an idea! thought Miggle. *Where's my fishing net? I'll get that and catch the jug in it. Then I'll smash it to bits on the ground. Oh, this treacle! How I hate walking in it! It's just like glue!*

He made his way to the corner where he kept his net and took hold of it. At once the Treacle Jug swung itself over to him and poured treacle down on his head and face. How horrible! How sticky! Miggle was so angry that he shouted at the top of his voice. I imagine the whole of Goblin Village heard Miggle as he shouted louder and louder! Miggle was an extremely angry little goblin. He started shouting at the Treacle Jug again.

'I'll smash you! I'll break you into a hundred pieces!

I'll teach you to pour treacle all over my house! You just wait!' He swung the fishing net at the jug and almost caught it. It seemed frightened and swung away out of the door and up the stairs, pouring treacle all the way. Miggle sat down and cried bitterly. His house was in a mess and most of his things were ruined. And he was covered from head to toe in sticky treacle. Whatever was he to do?

Soon he heard a curious glug-glug noise, and he looked up in alarm. A river of treacle was flowing slowly down the stairs! It flowed through the kitchen and out of the door, down the path and into the street. People passing by were quite astonished. They had never seen a river of treacle in Goblin Village before. 'It seems to be coming from Miggle's cottage,' said one man. 'How strange!' said his friend.

More and more people gathered to watch the treacle river flowing down the street. They stood around shaking their heads and muttering in astonishment.

Mother Tick-Tock, coming back from visiting her friend, was astonished too. But she knew in a trice what had happened.

'Miggle's borrowed my Treacle Jug!' she said. 'I saw him peeping through the window when I used it the other night. The mean, thieving little fellow! That goblin just can't help himself; he is always getting into mischief. I knew he was up to no good when I saw him at my window.'

Miggle saw Mother Tick-Tock and waded out through the treacly river to his front gate, crying, 'Please, Mother Tick-Tock, I'm sorry. I can't make the jug stop pouring. Is there a spell to stop it as well as to start it?'

'Of course there is,' said Mother Tick-Tock. 'It's just as well to know both spells if you steal something like a Treacle Jug, Miggle. Well, you can keep the jug if you like. I've a much bigger one I can use. How tired of treacle you must be, Miggle!'

'Oh, Mother Tick-Tock, please, please take your

jug away,' begged Miggle, kneeling down in the treacle. 'My house is covered in treacle. There is treacle all over the kitchen table. There is treacle all over my armchair. My new hearth rug is covered in treacle. I am covered in treacle! Look, even the street is covered in treacle. It's everywhere! Please can you make it stop? I'll do anything you say, if you only will!'

'Very well. If you come and dig my garden for me all the year round and keep it nice, I'll stop the jug from pouring, and take it back,' said Mother Tick-Tock. Miggle groaned. He did so hate gardening! It was so boring and such hard work.

'But your garden is so big!' he exclaimed. 'I shall have to spend all my time keeping your garden looking nice,' moaned Miggle.

'Well, I can always leave the Treacle Jug with you,' said Mother Tick-Tock.

'No,' said Miggle at once. 'Please take it away. I'll come,' he said. 'I don't want to, but I will.'

'If you don't, I'll send the jug to pour over your

head,' said Mother Tick-Tock, and everyone laughed. She called loudly, 'Treacle Jug, come here!'

The little blue jug sailed out of a bedroom window and hung over Miggle's head. He dodged away at once. The last thing he wanted was to get covered in more treacle! Mother Tick-Tock chanted loudly,

> *'Be empty, jug,*
> *and take yourself*
> *Back to your place*
> *upon my shelf!'*

And – hey presto – the Treacle Jug became quite empty, turned itself upside down to show Mother Tick-Tock that it had obeyed her, and then flew swiftly through the air on the way to her cottage. Mother Tick-Tock knew she would find it standing quietly in its place on her kitchen shelf.

'I will give my children bread and treacle for their supper tonight now that the Treacle Jug has been returned to its proper home,' said Mother Tick-Tock.

What's this? Miggle has turned rather a strange colour upon hearing the word 'treacle'!

Mother Tick-Tock laughed at the funny look on Miggle's face. 'Well, goodbye, Miggle,' she said. 'You've quite a lot of cleaning up to do, haven't you? Somehow I don't think you'll want to eat treacle again in a hurry!'

She was right. Poor old Miggle can't even see a treacle tin now without running for miles! And I'm not a bit surprised at that!

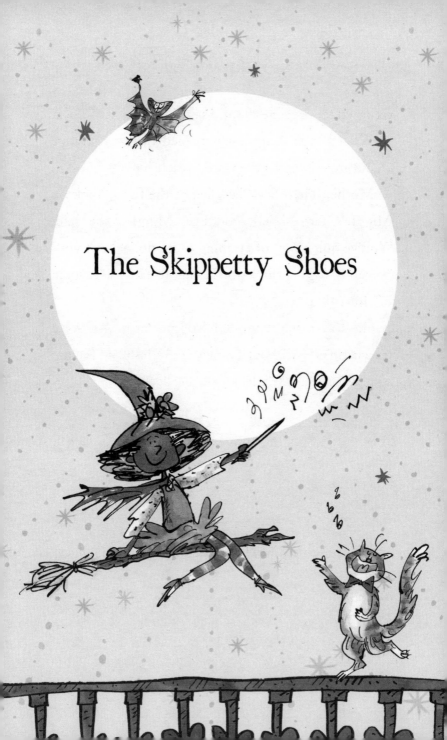

The Skippetty Shoes

The Skippetty Shoes

MR WINKLE was a shoemaker. He lived in a tiny, tumbledown cottage, and all day long he sat outside on a bench and made or mended shoes. He was a merry, mischievous fellow, always ready for a joke. Sometimes he played naughty tricks and made his friends cross.

One time he ran a glue brush inside a pair of shoes that he sold to Father Grumps – and dear me, how Grumps tugged and pulled to get those shoes from his feet! In the end both his socks came off too, and Father Grumps was very angry indeed.

Another time Winkle put a squeak into the heels

of some boots he sold to Dame Twisty, and when she heard the squeak-squeak-squeak as she walked, she really thought it was a goblin coming after her, and she fled down the street in fright, her shoes squeaking loudly all the time! Yes, really, Mr Winkle was a mischievous fellow.

He got worse as he grew older, instead of better. People shook their heads and said, 'One day he will go too far, and then who knows what will happen to him?'

Now, one morning, as Mr Winkle sat mending shoes, and humming a little song that went, 'Tol-de-ray, shoes for a fay, tol-de-rome, shoes for a gnome,' a gnome came by. He stood and watched Winkle at work, and Winkle looked up and grinned.

'You've a lot of time to waste!' he said cheekily.

The gnome frowned. He felt in his bag and brought out a pair of old slippers, each of which had a hole in the sole. They had once been grand slippers, for there was a gold buckle on each, and the heels were made of silver.

'How long will you take to mend these?' asked the gnome.

'One hour,' answered Winkle, looking at them. 'My, how grand they were once – but they are very old now, and hardly worth mending.'

'They are most comfortable slippers,' said the gnome, 'and that is why they are to be mended, Mr Winkle. Now, set to work, and keep your tongue still. It wags all day long.'

'Better than growling all day long, like yours!' answered Winkle cheekily. The gnome frowned again, and sat himself down on a stool.

Winkle tried to make him talk, but he wouldn't say a word. He just sat there and thought.

Mr Winkle felt annoyed. What an old solemn face the gnome was! *Cross old stick*, thought Winkle, as he began to mend the slippers. His needle flew in and out, and his busy little brain thought about the old gnome.

Presently an idea came into his naughty mind. He would play a trick on the gnome. But what trick could he play? He thought and thought and then he got up and went indoors. Somewhere he had got a little Skippetty Spell – but where was it? If only he could find it, what a fine trick he would play on the old gnome!

He hunted here and he hunted there – and at last he found it, tucked inside a milk jug. Good! Winkle hurried back to his bench, and found the gnome looking crossly at him.

'Where have you been?' he said. 'Get on with your work. I want those shoes finished at once.'

Winkle made a face and sewed quickly at the shoes. Into each he sewed half of the Skippetty Spell, grinning to himself as he thought of how the gnome would kick, jump, leap and prance, as soon as he put those slippers on his feet. Ho, ho! That would be a funny sight to watch! That would teach the solemn old fellow to frown at him and talk crossly!

'The slippers are finished,' said Winkle at last. He handed them to the gnome, and took his payment.

But still the old fellow sat there on his stool, as if he were waiting for someone.

'What are you waiting for?' asked Winkle.

'The king is coming to call for me here,' said the gnome. 'He said he would fetch me in his carriage. It is his shoes you have mended. They're his oldest ones, but so comfortable that he cannot bear to get new ones.'

Winkle stared in horror. Gracious goodness, were they really the king's own slippers? He was just going to take them from the gnome when there came the sound of galloping hooves, and up came the king's carriage. The gnome stood up and went to the gate. The carriage stopped and the king leant out.

'Did you get my shoes mended?' he asked.

'Yes, Your Majesty,' said the gnome and gave them to the king. His Majesty kicked off his grand gold boots and slipped his feet contentedly into his old slippers.

'Oh, how nice to have these again!' he began –

and then he stopped in dismay. Oh, those slippers! As soon as they were on the king's feet the Skippetty Spell began to work, and what a shock they gave His Majesty!

They jumped him out of the carriage. They made him kick his legs up into the air. His crown fell off into a lavender bush, and his cloak was shaken all crooked. He pranced round the garden, he kicked high, he kicked low, he jumped over the wall and he spun round and round till he was quite giddy. Certainly that Skippetty Spell was very powerful indeed!

The gnome stared at the king in horror. Mr Winkle turned pale and trembled. When the gnome saw Winkle's face he knew that he must have played a trick. He was full of rage and he caught the trembling cobbler by the collar.

'What have you done to the king's slippers, you wicked creature?' he shouted.

'There's a Sk-Skippetty Sp-Spell in them,'

stammered Winkle. 'Do you know how to get it out? I don't!'

Luckily the old gnome was a clever fellow, and he knew how to deal with a Skippetty Spell. He clapped his hands seven times, called out a strange magic word and hey presto the spell flew out of the slippers, they stopped dancing and the king sat down to get his breath.

Mr Winkle knelt down and begged the king's pardon – but he was far too angry to listen.

'Take your tools and go away from Fairyland!' roared the king. 'I've a good mind to turn you into an earwig, you mischievous little creature! Go away before I think of the right word!'

Winkle was in a terrible fright. He was so afraid of turning into an earwig that he caught up his bag of tools then and there and fled right away. He ran until he came to the borders of Fairyland, and not till then did he feel safe. He kept looking at himself, to see if he were Winkle, or an earwig.

Now he lives in our world. He still makes shoes for the pixies – very tiny ones, gold and black. He has no shop now, so he has to store them somewhere else – and do you know where he puts them? I'll tell you.

Find a white dead-nettle blossom and lift up the flower so that you can peep inside the top lip. What do you see there? Yes – two pairs of tiny pixie slippers, hung up safely by Mr Winkle the cobbler!

Aren't they sweet? Don't forget to go and look for them, will you?

Susie and Her Shadow

Susie and Her Shadow

ONCE A very funny thing happened to Susie. She was sitting in the sunshine, reading a book, when she saw a small pixie running by her with a big pair of scissors.

Susie was so surprised to see a pixie that at first she couldn't say a word. She just stared and stared. The pixie spoke first.

'Hallo!' he said. 'I suppose you don't really want your shadow, do you?'

'Whatever do you mean?' cried Susie.

'Well,' said the pixie, 'I'm just asking you if you want your shadow. It's no use to you. It would be *very* useful to me, if you'd let me have it.'

'But what do you want a shadow for?' asked Susie.

'Well,' said the pixie, whispering, 'you see, it's like this. I know a spell to make a magical cloak. If anyone puts on this magic cloak they will not be seen – they will be quite invisible. And I *do* want a magic cloak!'

'But what's a shadow got to do with a magic cloak?' asked Susie in surprise.

'You are *silly*,' said the pixie impatiently. 'The magic cloak is made of somebody's shadow, of course. That is why I want your shadow.'

'But I want my shadow too,' said Susie.

'Now don't be silly and selfish,' said the pixie, opening and shutting his big scissors. 'What use is your shadow to you? Does it play with you?'

'No,' said Susie.

'Does it help you to do your lessons?' said the pixie.

'Of course not,' said Susie.

'Well, then!' cried the pixie. 'What's the use of it? None at all! You might just as well let me have it.'

'Why don't you cut your *own* shadow?' said Susie suddenly. 'If my shadow is no use to me, then yours is certainly no use to *you*! You *can't* have my shadow, pixie, so now you know.'

Then the pixie fell into a tremendous rage and stamped about and shouted. Susie was a bit afraid at first, and then he looked so funny that she couldn't help laughing.

'Oh! So you're laughing at me, are you?' cried the little fellow in a rage. 'Then I'll steal your shadow without waiting for you to say yes!'

And with that he opened his big scissors and began to cut all round poor Susie's shadow. Of course it didn't hurt her, but it was dreadful to see her pretty purple shadow being cut away behind her. She tried to stop the little pixie, but he was too quick. With three or four snips of his sharp scissors he had cut off the whole of Susie's shadow.

Then he neatly rolled it up, put it over his shoulder, laughed loudly and ran off. Susie ran after him.

The pixie ran to a rabbit burrow and disappeared down it. He was gone.

Susie began to cry. She looked behind her. She had no shadow at all, not even the tiniest one, and it was strange to be without her shadow.

'I don't feel right without my shadow,' she wept. 'And how everyone will laugh at me. They'll call me The Girl Without a Shadow!'

She was so busy crying and wiping her eyes that she did not see a magical brownie looking at her from his house in a tree. He had opened his door, which was cut in the trunk, and was looking very puzzled.

'Little girl! Whatever's the matter?' he called at last. 'You are making such a noise that I can't hear my radio.'

Susie had already had so many surprises that she hardly felt astonished at all to see a magical brownie looking out of a treehouse at her. She wiped her eyes and answered him.

'Well, *you'd* cry too, if you'd just had your shadow

cut off by a mean little pixie who wanted to make a magic cloak with it!' said the little girl.

'Good gracious!' said the magical brownie, stepping out of his tree and looking closely at Susie. 'You are quite right. You haven't a shadow. Well, well, well!'

'It isn't well at all,' said Susie. 'It's perfectly horrid. I simply dón't know what to do. The pixie went down this rabbit hole, and I'm too big to follow him.'

'I can help you,' said the magical brownie. 'Come inside my treehouse and you can go down to my cellars. They lead into the passage to the pixie's home, just near the rabbit burrow.'

'Oh, thank you,' said Susie. She climbed into the treehouse after the magical brownie. She had hardly time to see what it was like, because the magical brownie took her so quickly down some winding steps right to his cellars. He opened a door there, and Susie peered out into a dark passage.

'Where do we go from here?' she whispered.

'Follow me,' said the magical brownie. He led the

way down the passage till they came to a door marked
MR PIXIE PODGE.

'This is where he lives,' said the magical brownie.
He hit the door with his fist and it flew open. Susie
stared inside.

She saw a small room, just like a cave. From the
rocky ceiling hung a bright lantern. Underneath it
sat the naughty pixie, sewing away at Susie's purple
shadow. He looked up in surprise as the door
flew open.

'So you stole this little girl's shadow, did you?' said
the magical brownie in a fierce voice. 'Another of your
bits of mischief, Podge! Give it back to her at once.'

'Shan't!' said the pixie, and in a trice he flung the
purple shadow round his shoulders like a cloak. At
once he disappeared!

'There! He's gone!' said Susie. 'He told me that a
shadow would make a magic cloak, and it was true.
Now what are we to do?'

'We can't get your shadow back, that's certain,'

said the magical brownie, puzzled. Then he grinned. He caught up the pixie's large pair of scissors, which were on a nearby table. He ran to the other side of the lantern where a blue shadow lay on the floor.

'Look!' said the magical brownie. 'The pixie has disappeared all right – but his shadow hasn't! I'll cut it off, and give it to you.'

Before the pixie could run away, the magical brownie had snipped three times with the scissors – and the pixie's shadow was cut off. The magical brownie rolled it up and gave it to the surprised little girl.

'There you are!' he said. 'He took *your* shadow – now you've got his!'

'But how can I put it on me?' asked Susie in dismay. 'I can't possibly!'

'Dear, dear! What a fusser you are!' said the magical brownie. 'Come back with me and I'll see what I can do for you.'

So, leaving the little underground room, where

they could hear the pixie crying, although they could not see him, the two went back to the treehouse. The magical brownie found a workbasket, threaded a needle with blue cotton and then took the shadow from Susie. He made her stand up, and then he neatly fitted the shadow's feet to her own feet. He quickly sewed it to her shoes with such tiny stitches that Susie couldn't possibly see them.

'There you are!' he said. 'That's done.'

Then he suddenly began to laugh. He laughed and laughed, and Susie got quite cross with him.

'Whatever's the matter?' she said.

'Well,' said the magical brownie, giggling, 'well, little girl, just look. You've got a pixie's shadow instead of your own. See the pointed ears! Oh, it's very funny!'

Susie looked round at her shadow. The magical brownie was perfectly right. She had a pixie shadow! Although she was a little girl, her shadow was that of a pixie. Susie suddenly felt very pleased.

'I'm glad,' she said. 'I'm glad. I know this isn't a dream now, because I've only got to look at my shadow and see a pixie's shadow, and I'll know it's all true! Oh, what fun!'

And off she skipped home, her pixie shadow following her and skipping too. I think she's lucky, don't you? Do you know a Susie? Well, have a look at her shadow next time you see her, and if it's like a pixie's, you'll know she's the same Susie as the one in this story!

The Cat that Could Sing

The Cat that Could Sing

THERE WAS once a big ginger cat called Thomas, who lived with his mistress, Dame Hoppity, in a small cottage at the end of Wallflower Village.

Thomas was a good mouse catcher, but Dame Hoppity forbade him to catch birds. He was a clever cat, and knew exactly what was said to him, so he seldom did catch birds – only just once and again. But what he really *did* want to catch was the canary that sang next door! It lived in a big silvery cage and sang loudly from morning to night.

'How I love to hear that bird!' Dame Hoppity would say, listening to the canary's song. 'I am so glad my next-door neighbour, Mr Tib, leaves his windows open. I couldn't hear the canary if they were shut.'

Thomas, the ginger cat, didn't at all like to hear the bird singing. It always seemed to begin just when he had made up his mind to have a good long snooze on the wall outside. Then, sure enough, the canary would start!

'Tirra-lirra, sweet, sweet, sweet, tirra-loo!' it sang loudly and brightly. 'Cheery-erry-erry, trilla true, trilla true!'

'Be quiet!' the big cat would hiss – but the canary hopped up and down in its cage and sang all the more loudly. Then Thomas would know he must leave the warm wall and go off into the potting shed right at the end of the garden, where he could hardly hear the canary. Bother!

One day Dame Hoppity saw him watching the canary angrily, and she knew that he wanted to catch it. So she warned him. 'Now don't you think of catching that canary, Thomas! It's half a magic bird, and you don't know what would happen to you if you ate it. Just take my advice now!'

But Thomas felt sure Dame Hoppity was just making it up to scare him, and he took no notice at all. He patiently waited his chance.

It came one fine day when Mr Tib had gone out and left the canary's cage on the windowsill. He usually took it indoors when he went shopping, because of the cats outside, but this time he forgot. Dame Hoppity was out too, so there was a fine chance for Thomas to get that nuisance of a singing canary!

He jumped over the garden wall. As soon as the canary saw him it set up a tremendous singing, and Thomas hissed angrily. He jumped at the cage, wrenched the door open and gobbled up the poor singing bird. Aha! That was the end of *him*!

Now he would pretend to know nothing at all about it. He lay down under a bush and went to sleep. What a disturbance there was when Mr Tib came back and found his canary gone! How he roared and stamped, and how upset Dame Hoppity was when he told her!

'I am sure it isn't my Thomas who has taken your canary,' she said. 'He always promised me he would never catch birds. Look at him, lying so peacefully asleep under that bush there. He would have run away if he had done a naughty thing like that!'

Thomas went in for his tea that afternoon, feeling sure that nobody would ever know what he had done.

'Hallo, Thomas dear,' said Dame Hoppity kindly. 'Do you want your tea? Fancy, that silly old Mr Tib thought you had taken his canary this afternoon! I soon told him what I thought of him!'

Thomas opened his mouth to mew, and then a dreadful thing happened! He began to sing! Yes, he did, just like a canary! You should have heard him! 'Trilla true, tirra-lirra!' he warbled, just as the canary used to do.

Dame Hoppity stared at him in alarm.

'What is the matter?' she asked, stroking the cat gently, wondering why he made such funny noises.

Thomas tried to purr – but goodness me, that awful singing came again! 'Tirra-lirra, sweet, sweet, sweet!' he sang.

Then Dame Hoppity knew that it was a canary's singing, and she guessed that Thomas had eaten the bird. It was half magic, and so Thomas's voice had changed to a canary's. Now he would have to warble and trill instead of mew or purr.

'Oh, Thomas!' she cried in horror. 'You ate that canary! Oh, dear, oh, dear! Now see what has happened to you! You had better come with me to Mr Tib and see if he can do anything about it.'

But Mr Tib was so angry when he heard that Thomas had eaten his canary that he would do nothing at all about it. Thomas fled, crying, 'Tirra-lirra, sweet, sweet, sweet!'

He went to the woods and tried to get his own voice back again, but no matter how he tried to purr or mew, all he could do was to warble and sing, just as the canary used to. As he sat under the trees trying his hardest to stop singing and mew instead, he heard someone laughing. He turned and saw old Witch Wumble, her black cloak flying out in the wind, laughing at him till the tears ran down her cheeks.

'A cat singing like a canary! Well, I never did! I suppose you've eaten old Tib's canary and have lost your voice and found another? Well, well, you were warned not to touch that magic bird! Serves you right!'

Thomas crawled to Witch Wumble and tried to mew to her to ask her to help him – but all he could do was to say, 'Trilla true, sweet, sweet!' very loudly. Still, she knew what he meant.

'I'll help you if you'll help me,' she said. 'Come and catch all the mice in my cellars, and all the rats too – then I'll help you to get rid of that singing voice and you can go back to Dame Hoppity's.'

Poor Thomas! Witch mice were difficult to catch

and tasted horrid, while as for the rats they were really fierce creatures, almost half as big as Thomas himself. But he really *must* get rid of his singing voice, or he would be laughed at all his life long!

It was difficult for a singing cat to catch rats and mice. Sometimes the trills would stop, and Thomas could lie by a hole and watch in silence for a mouse to come out – and then, just as he was about to pounce, his voice would start warbling loudly again and off would go the mice!

It took him three weeks to catch all the rats and mice, and as they tasted really very horrid, he didn't eat any of them. Witch Wumble wouldn't feed him, so he had to go and find what food he could, and he became very thin indeed. How he longed to be back at Dame Hoppity's with his creamy milk and his tasty fish! But he couldn't possibly go back with a canary's voice. Every cat, every dog, and even the birds and mice would jeer at him and call after him. No – he must just put up with things and hope that when his punishment was over Witch Wumble would do something for him.

She did. When she saw that every mouse and rat had gone, either caught by Thomas or fled through fear, she called him to her.

'Now you shall have your reward,' she said. 'I want your longest whisker, please, and three red hairs from your tail. I'll pull them out. Thank you!'

Thomas tried to mew with pain, but all he managed to say was, 'Tweet, tweet' and that made Witch Wumble laugh. She laid the hairs in a row on her table and took a yellow feather from a box. She laid it on top of the hairs and then said a strange and wonderful string of words over them.

Thomas felt his voice coming up out of his throat. It warbled more and more loudly, until he felt as if his throat was going to burst. The hairs and the feather stirred as if in a wind. Then suddenly a very strange thing happened! The hairs and the feather vanished and in their place stood – what do you think?

Yes, the canary! It preened its feathers and then, opening its yellow beak, it sang and sang and sang!

Thomas tried to mew in surprise – and to his great delight and astonishment he *did* mew! His canary's voice had gone – back to the real canary who had so marvellously come again. How thankful Thomas was!

'Now you must take this canary safely back to Mr Tib,' said the witch. 'I haven't a cage, so you must let it stand on your head and take it back like that. I know you won't ever try to catch it again, so it will be quite safe with you! Goodbye, and don't be silly again.'

The canary flew up on to Thomas's head and off the two went, a comical-looking pair, as you can imagine! How everyone laughed and stared to see the two! But Thomas didn't care. He was far too happy to bother about anything, for he had got his voice back, the canary was alive again, and he was going home, home, home to kind Dame Hoppity, to have creamy milk and tasty fish once more. Purrrr-rr-rr-rr-rr!

And after that, as you can imagine, Thomas *never* caught a bird again!

The Conjuring Wizard

The Conjuring Wizard

JIMMY WAS dreadfully disappointed. He had been asked to a party that day, and now here he was in bed with a cold! It really was too bad.

Mummy was very sorry for him. 'Cheer up, darling,' she said. 'There will be lots more parties.'

'Yes, but this one is going to have a conjurer,' said Jimmy. 'Just think of that, Mummy! Oh, I do wish I was going to see him.'

Mummy looked so sad to think that he was in bed, that Jimmy made up his mind to be cheerful about the party, and to pretend he didn't really mind. So he lay in bed smiling, and tried not to mind when he heard the children arriving at the party next door.

Mummy brought him his tea, and when he had finished it he lay back in bed, half asleep. Suddenly he heard a knock at the door, and he called out, 'Come in!' thinking that perhaps it was Jane, the maid.

But it wasn't. It was a strange-looking man in a high, pointed hat. He wore a cloak, and on it were stars and half-moons.

'Good evening,' he said to the surprised little boy. 'I heard you were not very well, so I came along to see you. Do you feel very dull?'

'It is a bit dull lying in bed with a cold when you know there's a party next door with a conjurer,' said Jimmy.

'A conjurer!' said the man. 'Do you like conjurers?'

'I should just think I do!' said Jimmy. 'Why, at a party I went to last year there was a conjurer who made some goldfish come out of a silk handkerchief and swim in a glass of water. And there was nothing in that handkerchief, because it was mine that I had had clean for the party!'

'Pooh, that's nothing!' said the strange-looking man. 'I can make goldfish come out of the pocket of your pyjamas and swim in your teacup!'

'You couldn't!' said Jimmy.

'Well, look here, then!' said the man, and he suddenly put his hand into Jimmy's pocket, took out three wriggly goldfish and popped them into the little boy's teacup, which suddenly became full of water. The fish swam about happily, then leapt up into the air and vanished.

'Ooh!' said Jimmy, astonished. 'How did you do that?'

'Aha!' said the man. 'I can do much cleverer things than that!'

'Then you must be a wizard,' said Jimmy.

'Perhaps I am,' said the man with a laugh. 'Just give me your handkerchief, will you?' Jimmy gave it to him. The wizard folded it neatly into four and laid it on the bed. 'There's nothing in it, is there?'

he said to Jimmy. 'Just feel and see.'

Jimmy felt. No, the handkerchief was quite soft and flat. The wizard picked it up and shook it out with a laugh. Out ran a white rabbit – and another – and another – and another!

'Goodness!' gasped Jimmy, amazed. 'However did they get there? Ooh, look at them running all over the room!'

The rabbits ran here and there, and suddenly popped up the chimney.

'They have gone,' said the conjurer. 'Now I'll do another trick. Open your mouth, Jimmy.'

Jimmy opened it, and to his great surprise the wizard began to pull coloured paper out of it. More and more he pulled, till the bed was full of it. Jimmy shut his mouth at last, and looked at the paper in astonishment.

'Well!' he said. 'I can't think how my mouth held all that, really I can't. Do another trick, Mr Conjurer.'

'I'll make the poker and shovel do a dance together,'

said the conjurer. He waved his hands, and suddenly the poker and the shovel each grew two spindly legs and two thin arms. Then they began to dance. How funny it was to see them! They bowed and kicked, jumped and sprang, and Jimmy laughed till the tears came into his eyes.

'Now do another trick,' he said.

Then the wizard did a strange thing. He picked up the coal scuttle and emptied all the coal on the bed!

'Oh, you mustn't do that,' said Jimmy. 'Mummy will be cross!'

'It's all right!' said the conjurer. 'Did you think it was coal? Well, it's not!'

And to Jimmy's great astonishment he saw that the lumps of coal had all turned into toys! There was a fine clockwork engine, a ship with a sail, a picture book, a box of soldiers and an aeroplane.

'Good gracious!' cried Jimmy. 'What fun!'

The wizard waved his hands once more. The engine leapt off the bed and ran round the floor. The ship jumped into Jimmy's washbasin and sailed there. The soldiers sprang out of their box and marched up and down the bed in a line. The aeroplane flew round and round in the air, and the book began to read the stories aloud!

'You are a marvellous man!' cried Jimmy. 'Do tell me who you are and where you come from.'

'Very well,' said the conjurer, and he sat down in the chair by Jimmy's bed. 'My name is . . .'

But just at that very minute there came another knock at Jimmy's door. The conjurer straightaway jumped through the window and vanished. The toys flew into the coal scuttle and became coal, and the coloured paper shrivelled up and disappeared in the twinkling of an eye.

The door opened and the doctor came in with Mummy.

'Hallo, hallo,' he said. 'And how are we feeling now?'

'He's looking better,' said Mummy. 'Why, Jimmy, you look quite excited. Anyone would think you had been seeing the conjurer after all!'

'And so I have!' said Jimmy. Then he told the doctor and Mummy all about the marvellous wizard. But they didn't believe him at all. And then Jimmy suddenly saw one of the rabbits! It came popping down the chimney and jumped up on the bed.

'You must believe me now, Mummy,' he said, 'for look, here's one of the rabbits!'

Jimmy still has that rabbit. Isn't he lucky?

The Flyaway
Broomstick

The Flyaway Broomstick

THERE WAS once a most annoying pixie called Poppo, who lived in Wobble Village on the borders of Fairyland. He was annoying because he was always borrowing things, and never returning them.

'It is such a nuisance,' said one small pixie to another. 'That naughty Poppo borrowed my only kettle yesterday, and now he says he didn't. So I have had to buy a new kettle!'

'And I had to buy a new set of dusters,' complained another. 'I hung mine out on the line, and Poppo came and borrowed them all without asking me. Then he said he never did, so I had to go out and spend all my money on new ones.'

'If only he wasn't so powerful,' sighed a third. 'But we daren't refuse him or scold him, because he knows more magic than any of us.'

'Yes, and do you remember how he turned little Sylfay into a worm because she told him he wasn't a borrower, he was a robber?' said the first one. 'We can't do anything, you know.'

But matters got so bad that the village knew they would have to do *something*. Poppo borrowed, or took without asking, all their nicest things. He would never give them back, and often said he had never had them at all. The little folk were in despair.

'I will go to the wise woman on top of Breezy Hill,' said Chippy, the leader. 'She will perhaps be able to help us.'

So he went off the next morning, and told his tale to the old wise woman. She listened, and for a time said nothing.

'You must be careful,' she said. 'This Poppo is

quite a powerful pixie.'

'I know,' sighed Chippy. 'But surely, oh wise woman, you can think of some way to stop him?'

The wise woman thought again. Then she smiled. She went to a cupboard, and took out a long broom.

'I have an idea,' she said. 'Take this broomstick home with you, Chippy. It once belonged to a witch and flies in the air. There is a fly-away spell hidden in it that will take twelve people for a flight and bring them back safely. But the thirteenth flight takes it to the witch it once belonged to, and she will keep for a servant the thirteenth rider.'

'Ooh!' said Chippy, frightened. 'Well, what are we to do?'

'Fly it in front of Poppo's house,' said the wise woman. 'Let twelve pixies, one after another, have a ride and then stop. Put it somewhere so that Poppo can borrow it – and if he doesn't fly off to the witch, then I am no wise woman!'

Chippy grinned in delight, and hurried off to

Wobble Village with the fine broomstick. He whispered all about it to the others, and in great glee they went to Poppo's cottage.

'I'll have first ride,' said Chippy. He sat astride the broomstick and waited. Suddenly it rose into the air, circled round the treetops, shot up high and then glided gently down to the ground again.

'Fine! Fine!' cried all the watching pixies.

'Someone else can have a turn now,' said Chippy. He slid off, and another pixie leapt on. Up rose the broomstick again, and away it went over the treetops.

When the fifth ride was being taken, Chippy saw Poppo looking out of his window, and grinned. Each of the pixies had a turn, but after the twelfth had been taken, Chippy stopped them.

'No more,' he said. 'It's teatime. We must all go home. I must take my broom into my backyard now, and use it for its proper purpose – sweeping!'

Off they all went. Poppo watched them go. He badly wanted a ride, but he wasn't going to say so.

No, he would go to Chippy to ask him for the loan of his broom, and say that he wanted to sweep out his backyard.

So after tea he put on his hat, and went round to Chippy's cottage. Chippy was watching for him, for he felt sure he was coming.

'Good evening, Chippy,' said Poppo. 'Would you be so good as to lend me a broom?'

'Ha, ha! You want to ride on it!' said Chippy, pointing his finger at him.

'Indeed I don't,' said Poppo, looking offended. 'I want to sweep my backyard.'

'Well, I warn you – if you ride on it, you'll be taken off to the witch who owns it!' said Chippy, who felt it would not be fair to let Poppo have the broom without a warning. 'No, Poppo – I think I won't lend it to you, after all.'

Poppo scowled, and went off. Chippy watched him. Soon the mean little pixie returned by the back way, creeping quietly into the backyard where he had spied the broom. He meant to take it without permission.

He ran off with it. Chippy whistled to his friends, and they all went softly after Poppo to watch what would happen.

'I said he wasn't to borrow it, and I warned him what would happen if he rode on it,' said Chippy. 'It will be his own fault if he is spirited away. He said he just wanted to sweep out his backyard.'

The pixies peeped over the wall. Poppo had the broom by the kitchen door, and he was looking at it carefully.

'All the other pixies had a ride, so I don't see why I shouldn't too,' said Poppo. 'That warning of Chippy's was all made up – he just said it so that I shouldn't have a nice ride like the others!'

He jumped on the broomstick. At once it rose into the air. It circled three times round the treetops, rose very high – and then went off like a streak of lightning to the west where the old witch lived!

'Ooh! He's gone!' cried the pixies.

So he had; and as he never came back, I suppose the witch took him for her servant, and he is probably there still. The pixies were delighted to be rid of him. They went to his cottage, and took away all the things that Poppo had borrowed and forgotten to return.

'Good old wise woman!' said Chippy. 'I'll bake her a cake this Saturday, and take it to her!'

He did – and she was simply delighted.

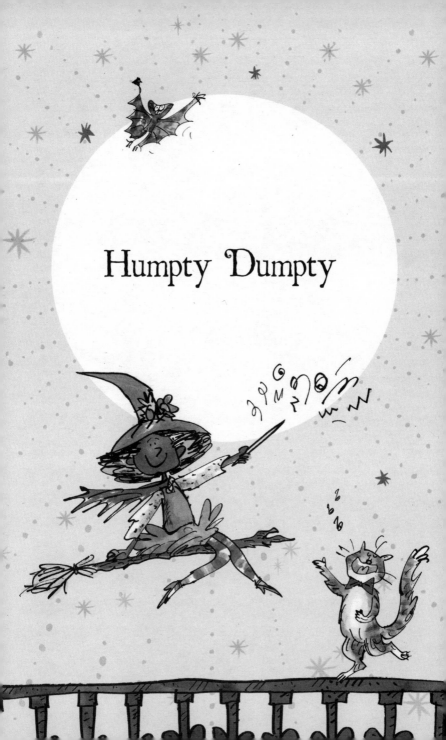

Humpty Dumpty

Humpty Dumpty

THERE WAS once a hen, who had given great help to a wizard. He was very grateful to her.

'I will do something in return for your help,' he said. 'Name your wish, and it shall be granted.'

'Sire,' said the hen, 'I do not wish all my eggs to grow into chickens. Grant that one of them may grow arms and legs instead of hatching to a chick!'

'So be it!' said the wizard, and waved his magic stick. 'Your next egg will grow arms and legs, and be able to talk. Only you must warn it not to climb any great heights in case it falls.'

That was how Humpty Dumpty happened. He

was a very large egg, and as he grew little arms and legs, and was able to talk, you may guess that all the countryside knew of him, and chattered about this extraordinary creature.

The hen was very proud of him, and one day, when the king passed by, she told him of her wonderful son. No sooner had the king seen him than he decided to take him to his palace, and let him live there.

For, thought he, *my little daughter will like him for a plaything*.

One day there was to be a great parade of all the king's horses and all the king's men outside the palace walls. Humpty Dumpty thought he would like to watch it.

'If I go and sit on the palace wall, I shall see beautifully!' he said to himself. 'And all the soldiers will see *me*, and think how wonderful I am!'

He forgot all about his mother's warning, and climbed up on to the wall and waved to the soldiers. When they waved back he was so pleased that he thought he would stand on the wall and bow to them.

But alas! Poor Humpty Dumpty overbalanced, and down he tumbled! Crack! He broke, for he was only a large egg, after all.

All the king's men on all the king's horses came galloping up in dismay, for they liked Humpty Dumpty.

They tried to mend the pieces of broken shell and put Humpty Dumpty together again – but, of course, they couldn't, any more than *you* can mend an egg that is broken. And sadly they went away and told his hen mother what had happened.

'Alas!' she wept. 'How foolish I was to wish him to be like men! If I had not been so foolish, dear Humpty Dumpty might be a fine chicken, alive and running about on legs like mine!'

Never since then has any hen wanted her egg to be anything else but chickens. And that, of course, is the reason why there has never been more than one Humpty Dumpty in history.

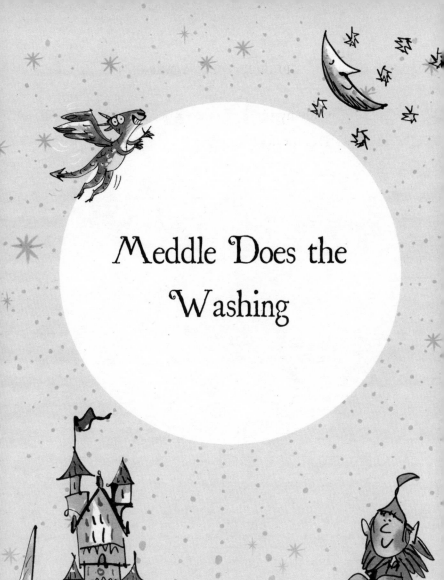

Meddle Does the
Washing

Meddle Does the Washing

MEDDLE WAS staying with his Aunt Jemima. He didn't like Mondays because it was his aunt's washing day then, and she groaned and grumbled all day long.

'Oh, how dirty you make your shirts, Meddle! Anyone would think you lived in a chimney! And look at these hankies of yours! Have you used them to wipe up spilt ink or something?'

'Oh, dear – it's washing day again!' Meddle would think. 'I must really get out of Aunt's way. She grumbles all day long – goodness knows why! There doesn't seem to be anything much in washing. You just get hot water, make a fine lather of soap and get on with it. I'm sure I could do it easily enough without any grumbling!'

He watched his aunt making the lather in the washtub. He liked all the bubbly, frothy lather. He dipped his fingers into it. It felt soft and silky.

'The better lather you have, the easier it is to wash the clothes,' said his aunt. 'But it's difficult to get a good, frothy lather these days. Get out of the way, Meddle. You'll have the tub over in a minute.'

Now, the next Monday, Meddle's aunt had a pain in her back. She sat in her armchair and groaned. 'Oh, dear, oh, dear! I can't do the washing today. I've such a pain in my back. I must do it tomorrow.'

Meddle looked at his aunt in alarm. 'Tomorrow! Oh, no, Aunt. You promised to take me to the fair.'

'Well, washing is more important than going to the fair,' said his aunt.

Meddle didn't think it was at all. He went into the scullery and looked at the pile of washing there.

Horrid washing! Now he wouldn't be able to go to the fair!

Then an idea came into his mind. Why shouldn't *he* do the washing? It always looked very easy. And if he got a really fine lather it would be easier still.

I'll go to Dame Know-All and ask her for a little growing spell, thought Meddle. *I'll pop it into the washtub with the lather, and it will grow marvellously so that I can do all the washing in no time at all.*

He went off to Dame Know-All. She was out. Meddle looked round her little shop. Ah – there on a shelf was a bottle marked GROWING SPELLS. Just what he wanted!

He put sixpence down on the counter, took down the bottle, unscrewed the lid and emptied a small growing spell into his hand. It was like a tiny blue pea.

He put back the bottle and went out of the shop. He ran back to his aunt's in glee. Aha! It took a clever fellow like him to think how to make washing easy!

What a fine soapy lather he would get. How all the dirt would roll out of the clothes when he popped them into the lather and squeezed them!

He peeped in at his aunt. She was still in her chair. She had fallen asleep. Meddle softly closed the door and went into the scullery. He filled the washtub with boiling hot water and popped in the soap flakes his aunt used. He swished them about with his hand, and a bubbly lather began to rise up in the tub.

Then Meddle put in the little blue growing spell. It dissolved in the water and made it bluer than before. A little blue steam came up and mixed with the soapy lather.

And the lather began to grow!

Hundreds and hundreds of soapy bubbles began to form in the tub, and frothed out over the tub, shining with all the colours of the rainbow.

'Good!' said Meddle, pleased, and he stuffed all the dirty clothes into the frothing lather. He pushed them down into the hot water, and began to squeeze them. But he couldn't do that for long, because the lather had grown so much that it frothed right up to his face. Bubbles burst and his eyes began to smart. He blew the lather away from his cheeks.

But it went on growing! He had taken a far too powerful growing spell from the bottle, and thousands and thousands of soapy bubbles were frothing up.

The lather fell out of the tub and went on growing. Soon Meddle was waist deep in bubbles! He kicked at them.

'Stop growing! That's enough! How can I possibly do the washing when I can't get near the tub? Stop, I tell you!'

But the lather didn't stop. It crept along the floor, frothing out beautifully. It grew higher. It sent bubbles all over the top of the table, and on to the gas stove. Gracious, what a sight!

Meddle began to feel alarmed. 'STOP!' he shouted. 'Don't you hear me? STOP!'

But bubbles went on growing by the hundreds and frothed about everywhere. Some of them rolled out of the window. The bubbly lather-stream went through the door into the kitchen. It frothed over the floor there, looking very peculiar indeed. Meddle began to get really frightened. He made his way out of the scullery, where the bubbles were now up to his neck, and found a broom. He attacked the lather with all his might, trying to sweep it back into the scullery, so that he could close the door on it.

But the more he swept, the quicker it grew! It was dreadful. Thank goodness the door into the parlour was shut. Whatever would his aunt think if she saw a mass of froth creeping into the parlour?

The larder door was open, and the lather went there, frothing all over the shelves. Oh, dear! It soon hid the meat pie and the cold pudding that Aunt Jemima had planned for dinner that day.

Aunt Jemima slept peacefully in the parlour. She had had a bad night and was glad to rest a little, with a cushion at her back. But when the noise of Meddle sweeping hard in the kitchen came to her ears, she awoke and sat up.

'What's that? What can Meddle be doing? The kitchen doesn't want sweeping!' she said to herself. She looked at the shut door and wondered if she should call out to Meddle to stop.

And then she saw something very peculiar indeed. A little line of lather was creeping under the door! A little drip of lather was coming through the keyhole! Aunt Jemima stared as if she couldn't believe her eyes. What was this strange thing creeping under the door? And whatever was coming through the keyhole? She wondered if she was still asleep and dreaming.

'Meddle,' she called, 'what are you doing? Open the door. There's something strange happening.'

Meddle heard what his aunt said – but he certainly wasn't going to open the door and let all the bubbles into the parlour! It was quite bad enough already in the kitchen. The froth was almost up to his shoulders. He couldn't even *see* his legs! Sometimes the bubbles went up his nose and made him sneeze and choke. His eyes smarted. He felt very upset.

Aunt Jemima watched the line of bubbles creeping under the door in alarm. As soon as the lather was properly in the parlour it began to grow very quickly. It frothed up into the air, and Aunt Jemima got out of her chair in fright. What was all this?

She trod through the bubbles and opened the door into the kitchen. That was a terrible mistake! At once a great cloud of soapy bubbles swept over her, and she was almost smothered in them. She screamed.

'Meddle, what *is* this? What's happening? Good gracious, I can hardly see the top of your head!'

'Oh, Aunt, oh, Aunt, it's all because of a growing spell I put into the washtub to make a fine lather!' wept Meddle. 'It won't stop growing now. Oh, what are we to do?'

'Well! Of all the donkeys, you're the biggest, Meddle!' shouted his aunt, trying to make her way through the bubbles. 'Open the garden door! Sweep the lather into the garden. Don't let it fill the house!'

Meddle groped his way to the door, coughing and sneezing. He opened it. A great wave of froth immediately rolled out. More and more followed. It went down the garden path, and all the passersby stood still in astonishment to see such a sight.

They had to get out of the way of the lather when it got to the hedge. It frothed over it and made its way down the road. Aunt Jemima watched it.

'Won't it ever stop?' said Meddle, really scared.

'It will stop when the growing spell is worn out,' said his aunt, in a very grim voice.

The spell didn't wear itself out for four hours. By that time the lather had reached the village, and all the children were paddling about in the bubbles, having a lovely time.

But at last the froth grew smaller and smaller. The

bubbles burst and disappeared and no more grew. By one o'clock there was not a single bubble left. The wonderful lather had gone.

Meddle was terribly hungry by this time. So was his aunt. She went to the larder and looked at the soapy meat pie and the cold pudding. Then she went out to the henhouse and found two new-laid eggs. She brought them back and put them in a saucepan on the stove to boil.

'You can have the pie and the pudding,' she said to Meddle. But when he tried to eat them he made a terrible face.

'Oooh! They taste of soap! Can I have an egg, Aunt?'

'There are only two, and I'm having them both,' said his aunt. 'Eat up the pie and the pudding.'

So poor Meddle had to, and they tasted far worse than any medicine he had ever had in his life.

'I shall have to do the washing tomorrow, just as I planned,' said his aunt. 'Next time you want to

meddle in anything, Meddle, tell me before you start.
It would save such a lot of trouble! As for the fair,
don't dare to mention it! It might make me put you
into the washtub with the dirty washing!'

Coltsfoot Magic

Coltsfoot Magic

'I KNOW a wonderful spell!' said Sly the gnome. 'One of the goblins who live under the mountain told me!'

'What's the spell?' asked his sister, Lightfoot.

'It's to make gold!' said Sly. 'I've always wanted to do that. It's coltsfoot magic. You know how golden the little coltsfoot flower is – well, if you know the right way, you can make a sack of gold from a hundred flowering coltsfoot!'

'Well – what would you do with the gold?' asked Lightfoot. 'Aren't you happy enough in our pretty little cottage? What would you do with a lot of gold?'

'I'd buy the house at the end of the village, the

one with a view over the valley,' said Sly. 'I'd turn out Old Mother Snow. I don't like her! And I'd buy up all the best things in the market for myself. And I'd get a horse to ride, and wouldn't I just gallop about the countryside, making everyone get out of my way!'

'You're not liked very much now,' said Lightfoot, 'and I think you'd be liked even less then. You're not a nice enough person to be rich, Sly. Only good people should ever have money and power.'

'Don't be so rude,' said Sly angrily. 'I tell you this, Lightfoot – when I make my coltsfoot gold I'll turn you out and get someone who doesn't say impolite things to me, as you do!'

'You are unkind, Sly,' said Lightfoot. 'I am your sister, and I love you, even though you are often unkind and do wrong things. If you could make people happier by being rich then I would help you. But why should having money make you want to turn Old Mother Snow out of her home, and buy the best things in the market for yourself? No, no – I don't like this coltsfoot spell of yours!'

Sly went out angrily and slammed the door. He shouted for Flighty, the goblin boy who dug his garden for him.

'Flighty! Come here! I've got a job for you to do. Go and pick me one hundred fine coltsfoot flowers – you know the ones I mean. They have round yellow heads a bit like dandelions, and scaly stalks.

'But they're not yet out, sir,' said Flighty.

'Well, as soon as they spring up and flower, bring me one hundred, with their stalks, and bring me one hundred of the leaves too,' said Sly. 'I need the leaves for my spell, as well as the flowers.'

Lightfoot heard him giving Flighty his orders. She was sad. Now Sly would become rich, and he would be horrider than ever. He would make people unhappy. But how could she stop him? She went out to visit her friend, Dame Know-a-Lot. She told her all about it.

'Well, well, it's certainly a pity when people like your brother Sly get wealth and power,' said Dame Know-a-Lot. 'But I rather think, Lightfoot, that we can stop him making his spell!'

'How?' asked Lightfoot surprised.

'Well, he says he wants the coltsfoot flowers *and* their leaves,' said Dame Know-a-Lot. 'I believe we could prevent the coltsfoot from sending up its leaves till the flowers are dead!'

'*Could* we? But how?' cried Lightfoot.

'I know all the moles that live about the countryside,' said Dame Know-a-Lot. 'And I could send them tunnelling underground to find all the hidden coltsfoot plants. They could tell them to send up their flowers first, but to hold down their leaves till the blossoms are over! Yes, I think I could manage it! No flower wants to be used for wrong purposes!'

'You do that then,' said Lightfoot, pleased. 'I'm sure Sly wants the leaves as well as the flowers!'

He did, of course. He had to boil the flowers first

in sunshine and water, and then add the leaves one by one, chanting magic words as he did so. Then he had to dance round in a circle while the mixture bubbled high. When it died down, every coltsfoot flower would have turned into a golden coin! But when Flighty went to gather the coltsfoot flowers and leaves, he could find only flowers! Very puzzled indeed, he hunted everywhere – but no matter where he looked, he could find only flowers. Not one single coltsfoot leaf, with its cobwebby covering, could he find!

Sly was angry when Flighty came back with the flowers only.

'What use are they without leaves?' he stormed. 'I suppose I must seek them myself, you lazy, good-for-nothing rascal.'

He set off to hunt for coltsfoot leaves himself. But, of course, he couldn't find a single one either. It was all most extraordinary!

Lightfoot didn't say a word when he stormed and

raved about it. She just went quietly about her work. Sly grew angrier and angrier.

'Don't you realise that if I can't get the leaves at the same time as the flowers, I can't possibly make that gold spell?' he shouted.

'It will be a good thing if you don't,' said Lightfoot. 'Now stop storming about, Sly, and come and have your dinner. You are lucky to have a nice meal. Don't spoil it by stamping about the room and letting it get cold.'

'I shall try and make the spell without the leaves,' said Sly at last. 'I'll see what happens.'

'Now, Sly, you know it's dangerous to make a spell if you haven't got everything you need for it,' said Lightfoot. But Sly wouldn't listen to his sister. No – he began to make the coltsfoot spell without the leaves!

But, oh my goodness – it wasn't the same spell at all! To do the coltsfoot spell without leaves made a grow small spell! Lightfoot, who was eating her dinner and watching, suddenly gave a loud cry.

'Sly! Sly! Stop the spell at once! Something is happening to you! You're growing smaller – and smaller! Stop, before it's too late!'

In a terrible fright, poor Sly stopped the spell. But he had dwindled to a quarter of his size. Now he was only as big as a tall buttercup – and there was no way he knew of getting back to his right size again. What a state he was in!

'I'm sorry for you, Sly,' said Lightfoot. 'Now you are so small that even the children are taller than you. What a pity you meddled with a gold spell!'

Poor Sly! He stayed small all his life, and he was always frightened of everything, because now even the dogs were bigger than he was! They came running after him, and sniffed at him in surprise, and he didn't like it at all.

Better for him to be small and harmless than big and cruel, thought Lightfoot. *It's my fault he's gone small, because I meddled with the coltsfoot flowers and their leaves*

– but he would have been such a horrid fellow if he had become rich!

The curious thing is that to this day the coltsfoot flowers come up without their leaves! The leaves come much later. You watch and see!

Five Times Five
Are . . .

Five Times Five
Are . . .

LITTLE HOPPITTY hadn't had at all a good morning at school. Mr Rap was very cross with him because he couldn't say his five times table.

Hoppitty managed all right till he came to 'Five times five'. He *couldn't* seem to remember that they were twenty-five.

'Five times five are twenty-six,' he said.

Mr Rap rapped on his desk. 'You said that yesterday, Hoppitty. Now – tell me the right answer this time. What are five times five?'

'I *know* they are twenty-six,' said Hoppitty. 'It sounds right and it is right, Mr Rap.'

'Now listen,' said Mr Rap. 'Take twenty-six pencils out of my class pencil box. That's right – twenty-six. Have you got them and counted them? Now Hoppitty, if you are right, and five times five are twenty-six, you will be able to arrange five nice piles of five pencils, out of those twenty-six. But mind – you mustn't have any over.'

'That's easy,' said Hoppitty.

'If you can do that I will put you at the top of the class,' said Mr Rap. 'And that's a place you've never been in before. And if you're wrong – my word, I shall have quite a lot to say to you!'

Well, Hoppitty began to put the pencils into piles of five. He made five nice piles – and then he found he had one pencil left over. Bother! He began all over again – but, of course, no matter how he tried, he couldn't make five times five come to twenty-six – there was always one pencil left over.

'There you are!' said Mr Rap. 'What did I tell you? Five times five are twenty-five, not twenty-six.'

Poor Hoppitty! It was painful learning what five times five were. He ran home from school. But on the way home he passed a curious little caravan standing by the roadside, and he stopped. Who lived there? He had never seen the caravan before. It must just have arrived!

Hoppitty tiptoed up to it. The door was wide open. Nobody was inside. On the shelves around the caravan were arranged little bottles of all colours.

'Bottled spells!' said Hoppitty to himself. 'Ooooh – I must just read the labels!'

He was reading the labels when suddenly someone came up the caravan steps – and the door banged loudly. Hoppitty turned round in alarm.

A little goblin woman stood there, with eyes as bright as green glass. 'Ho!' she said. 'What's your name? Is it Peep-and-Pry? Is it Snoop Around? Is it...?'

'No, no, no – I'm just little Hoppitty!' said Hoppitty in a fright. 'Let me go. My mother is a wise woman, and she will blow a spell at you and make your caravan vanish like a puff of smoke if you keep me here!'

'She can't. I am much cleverer than she is,' said the goblin woman. 'Nobody is so clever as I am. There is nothing I can't do! You've seen my bottled spells – well, half the magic in the world is in those bottles!'

'My mother is cleverer than you,' said Hoppitty, beginning to tremble. 'She could ask you to do something you couldn't do. Let me fetch her.'

'Oh, no! You wouldn't come back!' said the goblin woman. '*You* ask me something. Surely such a clever woman as your mother must have a clever son. Can't *you* ask me something I can't do?'

'Turn into a dog!' said Hoppitty. 'That's very difficult!'

It wasn't difficult for the goblin woman! In a trice she vanished, and in her place came a very fierce-looking dog that growled at Hoppitty.

'Now turn into a – a – cucumber!' cried Hoppitty,

trying to think of something that didn't growl or look fierce. At once a long green cucumber lay shining on the floor. Most peculiar!

The goblin woman appeared in her own shape again. 'I like you,' she said to Hoppitty. 'I shall take you along with me. You can pull the caravan when my horse is tired.'

'No, no!' cried Hoppitty. 'Give me one more chance. I know something you can't do, I do, I *do*!'

'Very well – one more chance,' said the goblin woman. 'Quick!'

'Well, have you got twenty-six pencils?' asked Hoppitty.

'Of course not,' said the goblin woman.

'Well – potatoes will do, I suppose,' said Hoppitty, seeing a basket of them nearby. He counted out twenty-six. 'Now see these potatoes?' he said to the goblin woman. 'Well, you're to put them into piles of five for me. You won't be able to do it.'

'A baby could do that,' said the goblin woman,

and she quickly made five piles of the potatoes, five in each pile ... but there was one over, of course.

'Oh, you mustn't have any over,' said Hoppitty. 'That's not allowed. You must just have piles of five with no potatoes over at all.'

Well, the goblin woman tried and tried, just as Hoppitty himself had tried at school that morning. In the end she cheated and put four piles of five and one of six. But Hoppitty saw what she had done.

'You're a cheat!' said Hoppitty. 'Cleverest woman in the world indeed! What rubbish! Why, I expect all those bottle spells are just coloured water. I shall tell everyone you're not clever enough even to ...'

'Get out of my caravan!' said the goblin woman fiercely. 'Go on, get out. I don't want you. You've played some kind of trick on me. You're too clever! Get out before I empty a bottled spell over your head!'

Hoppitty fled down the caravan steps and didn't stop once till he was safely at home. My goodness, what a good thing Mr Rap had made him find out that five times five are twenty-five and never could be twenty-six! You just never know when a bit of knowledge will come in useful!

The Stolen Eggs

The Stolen Eggs

ONCE UPON a time the egg woman found that someone was stealing the eggs from her henhouse. She could not think who it could be, and although she did her best to keep watch, she always fell asleep after a few minutes – and in the morning some of the eggs were gone again!

So she went to Mr Mog, the old wise man who lived at the other end of the village. He listened to her tale, and promised that he would catch the thief for her.

'Where would you like to keep watch?' asked the egg woman. 'There is a field between my house and the henhouse, but as we have had so much rain, it is very damp. It would not do for you to hide there – and you cannot see the henhouse from my cottage.

'Don't worry,' answered Mr Mog. 'I shall not want to hide anywhere. I will catch the thief for you without leaving my cottage tonight!'

'You are very clever,' said the egg woman admiringly, and off she went.

Mr Mog went to a cupboard and took out a box full of the tiniest hooks you can imagine. He put the box into his pocket and strolled round to the field that lay between the egg woman's cottage and her henhouse. He hunted about for a little plant that was covered with small rounded green fruits. He emptied the tiny hooks over the little green fruits, muttered a spell so that they clung fast to the fruits, and then went home.

Now that night along came Sneaky, the lad from the farm. He had come to steal the eggs as usual! He went down the field to the henhouse – and as he went, the hooks on the little green fruits caught hold of his coarse woollen stockings, and the green fruits snapped off the plant and clung to the lad's legs. He felt nothing, of course – and soon he had sneaked into the henhouse and out again – and in his pocket were twelve brown eggs!

Next morning Mr Mog took a walk through the village, and, dear me, how he stared at everyone's legs! It made people feel quite uncomfortable – but Mr Mog was looking for something! And very soon he found what he was looking for!

Along came Sneaky, the farm lad, stumping by in his woollen stockings – and they were covered with the little green hooked fruits! Mr Mog knew at once that Sneaky had been across that field – and why should he go unless to steal eggs?

'Sneaky, I am just going to tell the village policeman that you have been stealing eggs,' said Mr Mog, speaking in a dreadful, deep voice, just behind Sneaky. The farm lad jumped almost out of his skin and turned as pale as the moon.

'No, no!' he begged. 'Don't do such a thing, Mr Mog! I'll never steal eggs again – and I'll give the egg woman half my wages each week till I've paid for the eggs I stole!'

'Very well,' said Mr Mog – and so it was settled. The egg woman never knew how Mr Mog caught the thief – but to this day that little plant has its fruits covered with hooks. Have you found any? It is the common goose-grass, or cleavers!

Four Little Wheels

Four Little Wheels

ONE OF the oldest toys in Jack's room was a small motorcar. It had been there as long as the teddy bear had, and he had come when Jack was one year old.

There was a little tin man at the steering wheel of the motorcar, and at night he drove his car round and round the room at top speed. Everyone got out of his way then, because it wasn't pleasant to be bumped into and yelled at and knocked over.

'Stop it, tin man,' Teddy would say crossly. 'Look where you are going. That's twice you've run over the monkey's tail tonight.'

'Well, he shouldn't leave it about so,' said the tin

man. 'He should hold it up in the air or tie it round his waist or something.'

The tin man wasn't always as cross as he sounded. He was a kind old fellow really, and the smaller toys could have a ride with him whenever they liked. He simply loved tearing along at top speed. It was the one joy of his life.

His car was looking rather old now. It had four tiny wheels, each with a little rubber tyre round it. The wheels had once been painted bright red, but now they were dented and didn't run very straight.

This made the motorcar wobble when it went round a corner. The tin man had tinkered about with them, but he couldn't mend them. He was always afraid one would come off.

There was another thing he was afraid of too. He knew his car was old. He knew it looked dreadful. And he knew that old toys sooner or later were thrown away. They went into what Teddy called 'The Land of the Dustbin'. The toys hated to think about that.

When anyone was cross with the tin man they always said the same thing to him, 'You'll soon be off to the Land of the Dustbin, you and your silly old car! It will serve you right for tearing round and round, running over tails, and knocking down dolls and skittles!'

Then the tin man would look at his old car and shiver a little. *Yes*, he would think to himself, *I'm so afraid that Jack will soon want to send me away to that dreadful land. I have heard that tea leaves live there too, and potato peel, and old newspapers and broken glass. I don't want to go to the Land of the Dustbin.*

'*I* shan't go to the Land of the Dustbin,' the old teddy bear would say proudly. 'I have often heard Jack say that he will never part with me, never. I'm quite safe.'

The tin man wished he was quite safe too. He was very upset one day when Jack's mother came into his room, looked into his toy cupboard and said, 'Oh, Jack, what a lot of broken toys you have! You really must put some into the dustbin soon.'

'Oh, Mum!' said Jack. 'There's nothing I can spare, *really*!'

'Well, what about this awful old car?' said his mother, picking up the little motorcar, tin man and all. 'Its wheels are almost off – the paint is gone. I'm sure you don't play with it any more. This is one of the first things that must go. Now, really, you must make a pile of your old broken toys and I'll pop them into the dustbin.'

So Jack cleared out his toy cupboard and put some of the things into a pile. There was a very torn book. There was a broken brick box and some odd bricks. There was a game of snakes and ladders, broken in half, and a tiny rabbit without any head or tail. And, oh, dear, there was the old motorcar with the little tin man.

'I don't like sending you away,' said Jack to the little tin man. 'But I suppose you are awfully old, and your car does look dreadful now. The wheels are loose too.'

The tin man stared miserably in front of him. When Jack had gone out of the nursery the toys crept out of the cupboard and went over to him.

'Bad luck, tin man,' said the little furry dog. 'We shall miss you.'

'I do wish you weren't going,' said the clockwork mouse. 'But perhaps it won't be so bad in Dustbin Land after all.'

'Don't talk about it,' said the tin man in a choky sort of voice. 'I'm sorry I ran over your tails, clockwork mouse and monkey. I'm sorry I knocked you down, furry dog. I'm sorry I frightened you so many times, tabby cat.'

Nobody came to take the pile of broken toys away that night. It stayed there in the corner of the nursery, the little toy motorcar on top, with the tin man looking miserably round at the toys playing on the carpet.

Suddenly outside the window there came a noise of high chattering. 'It's the pixies,' said the teddy bear, peeping out. 'Going off to dance or something, I suppose.'

There came a rapping at the window, and the monkey and the bear together managed to open it just a crack at the bottom. They didn't need to open it wide because the pixies were even smaller than the toys. A little pixie climbed in out of breath.

'I say!' she said in her little high voice, just like a bird's. 'A dreadful thing has happened.'

'What?' asked the toys, crowding round her.

'Well, my aunt, Flicker-Wings, is very ill and sent for me and my sister,' said the pixie. 'So we set off in our carriage, flying through the air, drawn by our big tiger moth. But suddenly a bat swept down and snapped at our moth! We beat it off, but it has hurt one of the moth's wings so much that it can't fly. We simply *must* get to my aunt tonight, so we came here to ask if you've got anything that can fly, so that we can borrow it for our carriage – an aeroplane, say.'

'No, we haven't,' said the teddy bear. 'But we could lend you the clockwork mouse if you liked, and he could drag your carriage over the ground. He can't fly in the air.'

'But our carriage hasn't any wheels,' said the pixie. 'It would go bump, bump, bump all the time, and we shouldn't like it a bit.'

'Couldn't we lend you some wheels to fix on it then?' said the furry dog excitedly. 'Train, how about you. Would you lend some?'

'No,' said the train. 'I'd go off the rails if I took off any wheels.'

'Well, what about you, wagon?' said the bear, turning to the wagon nearby. But the pixie shook her head at once.

'Those wheels are much too big,' she said. 'We should only want very small ones.'

A doleful voice called from the pile of rubbish. 'You can have the four wheels off my motorcar, pixie. They are loose, so you can easily get them off, and they are the right size. I shall never want them again. I'm going to the Land of the Dustbin.'

'Poor thing!' said the pixie at once. 'I'm sorry for you. But it would be an awfully good deed if you could let us have your four little wheels. They are just the right size.'

It wasn't long before the monkey and the teddy bear had them off. The tin man stared at them sadly. 'Well, I'm glad someone's going to be able to make use of them,' he said, with a sigh. 'I hope you'll manage to get them on your carriage all right.'

'Oh, we shall use magic to do that,' said the pixie. 'It will be easy. We'll use some magic to make them a nice bright colour too – bright blue, I think. My word, we *shall* have a fine carriage. Clockwork mouse, would you mind taking us to our aunt? Our carriage won't be very heavy to pull.'

'Of course I'll take you,' said the mouse. He went outside with the pixie. The teddy and the monkey went too, carrying the four old wheels with them.

'Hallo!' said the pixie's sister in surprise. 'What's all this?'

She was sitting in the carriage outside. It was on the grass. Nearby was a moth, stroking its hurt wing with its feelers. It was very sorry for itself.

'We'll leave you here till you feel better, moth,' said the pixies. 'We'll see our aunt, and then come back home this way, to see how you are. If you are no better, you will have to squeeze into the carriage with us, and the clockwork mouse will drag us all home together, in our little carriage with wheels.'

It was marvellous to see how quickly the four wheels were fitted on with magic. Just a wave of a wand and they were in their place under the carriage! Another wave of the wand and they turned a beautiful bright blue!

'As good as new!' said the clockwork mouse in surprise, putting himself in front of the carriage and letting the pixies harness him. 'Well – off we go!'

And off they went, the little mouse running

swiftly on his clockwork wheels through the night. The pixies had to wind him up three times, but that was all.

Their aunt was much better, and had got someone to look after her, so that was good. The pixies promised to come again tomorrow, and set off homewards, the little mouse going swiftly. 'Go back to where we left the tiger moth,' said one of the pixies. 'We must take him home if he isn't better.'

But dear me, the moth was quite all right! He was flying round and round, waiting impatiently for the pixies to come back. He was feeling jealous of the clockwork mouse – it was *his* job, not a clockwork mouse's, to draw the pixies' carriage!

'I'm better!' he called, as the carriage came near. 'Tell the mouse to go back home. And take off the wheels. They will be too heavy for me to pull along, for I am not so strong as the mouse.'

'Oh, we are glad you are better again,' said the pixies. They tapped each wheel with their wands and the wheels at once fell off. The clockwork mouse got out of the harness and the tiger moth took his place.

'Will you take the wheels back to the tin man, and thank him very much for us?' said the pixies. The mouse said he would. He waved goodbye with his tail, put the wheels in a row down his back, and squeezed himself under a door. He went back to Jack's room and everyone was glad to see him.

'The pixies sent back the wheels,' said the clockwork mouse. 'Here they are. They look quite new now, because they aren't bent or dented any more – and the pixies made them bright blue. Won't the tin man's car look smart!'

The teddy bear put the four wheels back on the car. The tin man was full of delight to see them looking so new and bright. '*What* a pity I shan't use them any more!' he said. '*What* a pity I'm going to Dustbin Land!'

The next day Jack's mother came to take the pile

of rubbish – and how she stared when she saw the little motorcar on the top. 'Look, Jack!' she said. 'This isn't the old car I meant. This one looks new – see the dear little blue wheels? You can't put this into the dustbin. Put it back into your toy cupboard and when you find the one I meant take it down to the dustbin.'

'I haven't got another one,' said Jack in surprise. 'This must be the same one – with new wheels. I'd know my old tin man anywhere!'

You should have seen the tin man whizzing round and round the room that night, in his little motorcar with its bright blue wheels! He was as happy as he could be – and so were all the toys. Even when he ran over the monkey's tail he didn't get scolded, and they all joined in his joyful song:

'I'm not going off to
Dustbin Land!
Oh, isn't it grand,

FOUR LITTLE WHEELS

yes, isn't it grand,
He's not going off to
Dustbin Land!'

The Magic Silver
Thread

The Magic Silver
Thread

ONCE UPON a time there lived a wizard called Deep-Eyes, who had one son called Ho-Ho, a baby boy who was twelve months old. Ho-Ho used to crawl about the wizard's workroom while Deep-Eyes was making his spells, and one day a dreadful thing happened.

Deep-Eyes was making a spell for a witch who wanted her apple trees to grow bigger and stronger. He mixed all kinds of things together, and put the mixture in a blue bowl to cool. He set it on a low table, and then took down one of his magic books to read.

The baby found the bowl and liked the look of the

golden, shining water inside. He suddenly took hold of it, jerked it into the air and spilt it all over himself! Then what a to-do there was!

Ho-Ho cried and licked the mixture that was running all down his face. It soaked his clothes and made him shiver. The wizard shouted aloud in dismay and ran to his little son. The mother came rushing into the room, and picked him up.

'What a silly you are to stand bowls of water about!' she said to her husband, the wizard.

'It wasn't a bowl of water,' said the wizard with a groan. 'It was a golden spell I had made for the witch who came to see me yesterday. Now it's all wasted!'

'A spell!' cried his wife in dismay. 'Good gracious, Baby has licked some of it! Will it do him any harm?'

'I shouldn't think so,' said the wizard. 'We must wait and see.'

Well, for a little while the wizard and his wife saw nothing wrong with their son. He grew well, and was soon twice as big as children of his age. Everyone said what a fine boy he was, and how strong he looked.

But as he grew older, he shot up so tall, and became so broad, that folk began to wonder.

'He's much too tall for his age,' said one to another. 'There must be a spell on him. Why, he's only five years old, and yet he's much taller than his father, Deep-Eyes.'

Deep-Eyes soon knew what had happened. The spell he had made to make the witch's apple trees grow bigger and stronger was acting on his little boy, and making him grow huge. Soon the wizard and his wife were quite afraid of Ho-Ho.

So very soon he was allowed to do just as he liked, and everyone in the town tried to please him out of fear. This was very bad for Ho-Ho, and he grew up selfish and unkind.

When he was twenty years old he was simply enormous. He reached up to the clouds and his feet were as big as a large field. His voice was louder than thunder, and he ate more food than a hundred men could eat at each meal.

Nobody knew what to do with him. The whole town had to find food for him, and if by chance he did not have enough to eat, he would stamp his great feet till houses fell to pieces and everyone shook and shivered in fear.

At last he stopped growing, but he was easily the biggest giant in the world, and the most selfish. Nobody knew what to do with Ho-Ho, for he would not work. He told everyone they must work for him, or he would smash the town to bits.

One winter it was very cold indeed, and Ho-Ho commanded the townspeople to build him a great castle. But though they tried their best they could not build one that reached to the top of the giant's head. So they decided that he would be better off in a deep cave under the earth.

'You will be warm there, Ho-Ho,' they said. 'The

frost will not reach you, and you will be sheltered from the wind. There is not enough stone in the kingdom to build a castle big enough for you, so you must be content with a cave. We will do our best to make it very comfortable.'

At first Ho-Ho wouldn't listen, and demanded his castle – but soon he began to think that he might indeed be very cosy in a deep cave, and he told the little people to find one for him.

They did not trouble to find one. They asked Deep-Eyes the wizard to make one for them, and he brewed a very strong magic, said seven strange words and emptied the magic on to the ground. Lo and behold, a cave opened beneath his feet large enough to hold a dozen giants in comfort.

'Ho-Ho should be very comfortable in such a large cave,' said the people. The giant had his bed put there, a chair and a table, and soon made himself cosy.

'If only we could keep him there for always!' sighed

the people. 'But in the spring he is sure to come out again, trample on our houses and frighten everyone till they shiver and shake.'

'Couldn't we manage to tie him up?' asked Twinkles, a small pixie.

'Pooh!' said the chief man of the town. 'What an idea! Who do you suppose is going to tie Ho-Ho up, I should like to know!'

'I might be able to,' said Twinkles. 'I could think of a plan, I'm sure.'

Everyone laughed loudly at him, and he went away rather red in the face. He packed his bag and caught the train to Fiddle-Dee, the village where a great blacksmith lived. Twinkles made his way to his house, and found the clever smith hard at work.

'Could you make me a steel chain so strong that it couldn't be broken by anyone in the world?' he asked.

'Easily!' laughed the smith. 'What will you pay me for it?'

'Well, I haven't any money at present,' said

Twinkles, 'but if you really *can* make me a chain that no one can break, I shall be rich, and will pay you what you please.'

The smith agreed, and at once set to work. For four weeks he laboured hard, and at the end of that time he showed Twinkles a steel chain so strong and heavy that the little pixie could not move even one link of it.

'That will never break!' said the smith proudly. 'You will have to hire fifty horses to carry it for you.'

So Twinkles got fifty horses, and they dragged the great chain behind them to the town. Everyone came out to see it, and Twinkles explained that he had brought it to bind Ho-Ho with, so that he would never be able to get out of his cave.

'We will pretend to Ho-Ho that it is all a game,' said Twinkles. 'Come along to his cave and we shall all see what happens.'

So everyone trooped off to the cave where the giant lived.

'Ho-Ho!' cried Twinkles, peering down. 'Are you as strong as you were? There are some who say that your strength is failing!'

Ho-Ho growled angrily.

'Prove it!' he said in a rage. 'I am stronger than any other giant in the world.'

'Well, here is a chain that surely even *you* cannot break!' said Twinkles, and he bade the horses gallop near.

Ho-Ho took one look at it and snorted in scorn.

'You may bind me as tightly as you please with a toy chain like that!' he said. 'I will snap it in a moment!'

This was just what Twinkles wanted. He called the strongest men of the town to him and very soon they were binding the giant tightly with the chain, and made one end fast to a great rock.

'Ha! You are bound now!' cried Twinkles in delight. 'You cannot get free, Ho-Ho!'

But the giant only smiled. He stretched himself

and pulled on the great chain. Snap, snap, snap! It broke in twenty places, and Ho-Ho was free once more!

Then all the people had to pretend to be full of wonder and delight, for they were afraid to let Ho-Ho know that they really *had* wanted to bind him fast. He smiled and laughed, thinking that they were all glad at his strength.

'Bring a bigger chain still!' he said. 'I'll show you what I can do! Why, I could break a chain twenty times stronger than that!'

'Oh, no, you couldn't!' cried everyone. 'You really couldn't, Ho-Ho!'

'Try me and see!' said the giant.

So off went Twinkles to the smith again, and told him what had happened.

'Make a chain twenty times as strong,' he begged him. 'Surely the giant cannot break that!'

'I am surprised he could break the other,' said the smith, marvelling. 'Well, I will make this new chain for you, Twinkles, but I cannot make it alone. I must get twelve other smiths to help me.'

So he sent for twelve brothers of his, all famous smiths, and the thirteen set to work to make a chain stronger than had ever been seen in the world before. In three weeks it was finished, for the smiths worked all through the night as well as by day. It took a thousand great horses to drag it along, and everyone ran by the panting beasts and cheered them on.

When Ho-Ho saw the enormous chain he looked rather solemn.

'Ha, ha!' said Twinkles, seeing him look doubtfully at the chain. 'This is twenty times as strong, and you said you could easily break it! But now that you see it, you are afraid, Ho-Ho! Fancy a great giant like you, the biggest in the world, being afraid! Well, well, we will not let you try to break it, we will take it back from where we brought it.'

But Ho-Ho did not like being laughed at. He took

another look at the chain, and then looked at his great arms.

'You may bind me!' he said in his thunderous voice. 'I am not afraid! You will see how easily I can snap your silly little chain in two!'

So a hundred strong men bound him, and made one end of the chain fast to the rock. Then everyone stood back to see what would happen. Ho-Ho took a deep breath, and then tugged hard at the chain. It held! He tugged again. Alas! It flew apart in six different places, and the giant was free!

Once again the people had to pretend to marvel at him, and to be glad that he had broken their chain. Ho-Ho smiled with pleasure, for he loved people to admire him. But he made up his mind not to be bound again, in case one day he could *not* get free.

'I am tired of this chain game,' he said. 'I will not be bound any more!'

Then everyone knew that it was no use to try to bind the giant, and very sadly they went away.

But still Twinkles did not give up hope.

If thirteen strong smiths cannot help me, maybe one clever elf can get me what I want! he thought. So he packed his bag again and took the train that ran deep underground to the caverns of the mountain elves. Soon he came to where Peer-About, one of the very cleverest of the elves, had his home.

Peer-About had so much knowledge inside his head, that it had grown very big, while his arms and legs had remained small; so he was a strange-looking little person but kind-hearted and always willing to help anyone.

Twinkles told him all about Ho-Ho, and how he had broken the two chains.

'I suppose you can't help me?' he asked.

'I think I can,' said Peer-About, after he had thought for a moment. 'Stay here for a week, and I will give you something that no giant, were he as big as the world itself, could break!'

So for a week Twinkles stayed with Peer-About

in his little underground cave, and watched him work. The elf took the oddest things and mixed them all in a pot together. He took the footfall of six tigers, a little of the arch of a rainbow, some water from a bottomless pool and the roots of a high mountain. Many other things he took too, that Twinkles did not know, and carefully he stirred them all up together, chanting such strange words as he did so that Twinkles felt the hair standing up on his head with fright.

When the mixture was ready the elf put his hands into it and then drew them out again. The stuff clung to them like wet toffee, and the little elf wound it neatly round a pointed stick. It looked like glistening silver thread, no thicker than sewing-cotton on a reel. Peer-About wound it steadily round his stick, and at last there was nothing left in the bowl.

'Now I must put it out into the moonlight for one night,' he said, 'and it will be ready.'

'But, Peer-About, do you really think it will be

strong enough?' asked Twinkles. 'Why, it looks so slender I feel I could snap it myself!'

The elf smiled and said nothing. All that night the stick of silver thread lay out in the moonlight, and in the morning Peer-About made it into a small, gleaming ball of thread, and gave it to Twinkles.

'No one in the world can break that,' he said. 'Not even I, who made it, can snap it in two!'

Twinkles thanked the elf, and set off back to his own land. When he arrived there he showed his friends what he had been to fetch and they all laughed at him. They unwound the thread and pulled it – but no matter how they tugged and twisted they could not break it.

'But surely Ho-Ho will be able to snap it easily!' said everyone. 'It is so slender and so thin. And how are we going to bind him with it? He said he would not be bound any more.'

'I have an idea,' said Twinkles. 'It is springtime now and Ho-Ho will expect to leave his cave and come out into the sunshine again. We will bind daisies all along the thread as if it were a daisy-chain and take it to him, pretending that we wish to deck him and lead him out into the sun. Then we will bind him tightly with it, and he will not be able to move!'

'Well, we will try,' said the little people doubtfully. 'But we think that Ho-Ho will easily snap such a frail thread.'

Then everyone worked hard and picked hundreds of starry daisies, tying them prettily along the silver thread, so that it looked for all the world like a mile-long daisy-chain. When it was finished they went dancing and singing to the cave where Ho-Ho dwelt, as if they were full of joy at the springtime.

Ho-Ho looked up in surprise.

'We have come to fetch you out into the sunshine, Ho-Ho,' said Twinkles. 'And see! We have made up a lovely daisy-chain! Will you have it round you?'

Ho-Ho put out his hand and felt the daisy-chain, wondering if there was a strong chain hidden among the flowers. But when he felt the slender silver thread he smiled, for that was nothing, he thought.

He allowed Twinkles to wind the daisy-chain round and round him, and then the pixie deftly tied one end to the great rock inside the cave, making it fast.

'Now come, Ho-Ho,' he said, skipping nimbly out of the cave. 'Come out into the sunshine, decked with daisies!'

Ho-Ho stood up and tried to move forward, but the silver thread held him to the rock. He tugged lightly, thinking that the daisy-chain had become entangled in something, but still he was held fast. In a temper he pulled hard, but it was of no use – he could not get away.

Then Ho-Ho knew that he had been tricked, and he roared so loudly that chimney pots shivered on their roofs and nearly fell off. All the little folk fled away in a panic, stuffing their fingers into their ears. Ho-Ho tugged at the thread again and again, amazed that such a slender thing should hold him so tightly.

The daisies fell off one by one, and the giant twisted the thread round his great fingers.

But try as he would he could not snap it. It was far stronger than either of the chains. It slid through his fingers, and he could get no grip on it.

Then he knew he was caught and he roared aloud again in rage. He stamped his enormous feet and the earth shook. He banged on the cave walls with his fists, and the roof became so shaken that it dropped huge stones on to Ho-Ho's head, and made him angrier still.

All that day and all the night the giant roared and raged, while the people of the town crouched in their houses, wondering what would happen to them if the silver thread snapped in two. Only Twinkles was unafraid, for he knew what things it was made of.

Next day he went to the giant's cave and peered down into it.

'Listen to me, Ho-Ho,' he said sternly. 'You are bound here for ever, but it is your own fault, for you are an unkind and selfish giant, of no use to anyone. If you are quiet and peaceful, we will feed you each day.'

Ho-Ho listened and knew that he was defeated. He lay down quietly, and begged Twinkles to send him some food, promising to be good if only he might have something to eat.

Off went Twinkles, and soon all the people in the town had heard the great news – the biggest giant in the world was imprisoned and bound, and could never get away. How they cheered Twinkles and clapped him on the back! They gave him one hundred sacks of gold, and he at once paid the thirteen smiths who had tried so hard to make chains strong enough for Ho-Ho.

Then with the rest of the money he bought a fine little cottage, got married and settled down happily ever after.

As for Ho-Ho, he is usually quiet enough – but sometimes, when the little people bring him food he doesn't like, he gets into one of his old rages. Then he roars and bellows, stamps and kicks, and somewhere in the world there is an earthquake!

But you needn't be afraid that Ho-Ho will ever escape – the little silver thread that Peer-About the elf made will hold him fast until the end of the world!

Pippitty's Joke

Pippitty's Joke

PIPPITTY WAS a pixie – but what a naughty one. The things he did! He stuck a stamp on the pavement, and watched everyone trying in vain to pick it up! He put a parcel in the gutter, and when the passersby bent to see what it was it suddenly jerked away and made them jump – for Pippitty had got a black thread tied to it, and he was holding the other end round the corner.

When he got caught by Mother Go-Along, she told him off so hard that he cried a whole bucket of tears.

'I'll pay you out for this!' said Pippitty, and he ran off home. When he got there he wondered how he could play a trick on Mother Go-Along without her knowing that it was he who was doing it.

And at last he thought of a joke. 'I'll fly up to her roof – and take a can of water with me – and sit by her chimney – and pour water down it on to her fire! Then it will sizzle and smoke and she'll think someone has put a spell on it and will be so frightened!' chuckled naughty Pippitty to himself.

Well, he waited till night came. Then up to the chimney he flew, carrying with him a big can of water. He knew which was the kitchen chimney, for smoke was coming from it. My word, Mother Go-Along must be having a good fire, for the smoke was simply pouring out!

Pippitty grinned to himself. He sat on the edge of the chimney and tipped up the heavy can of water. Splishy-splashy-splishy-splashy – it hurried down that sooty chimney to the fire below!

Mother Go-Along was sitting in her rocking chair by the fire, knitting peacefully. Suddenly as a trickle of water reached the flames, the fire gave a loud sizzle-sozzle-sizzle, and sent out a cloud of black smoke!

'Good gracious!' said Mother Go-Along in alarm. 'What's all this?'

She poked the fire – it burnt up again after a while, so Mother Go-Along sat down once more to do her knitting. Flames shot up the chimney.

It was nice and warm.

Pippitty, sitting up on the roof, thought it was time to send down another lot of water – so he tipped up the can. An extra big lot went down – splishy-splashy-splishy-splashy! It reached the fire.

'SIZZLE-SOZZLE-SIZZLE-SOZZLE!' What a noise the fire made when the water tried to put it out! Mother Go-Along jumped up in fright. Clouds of dark smoke billowed out into her kitchen.

'It's a spell someone has put on my fire!' she cried. 'Yes – a spell!'

She cried this out in such a loud voice that Pippitty heard it, up on the roof. He grinned and chuckled and nearly fell off the chimney in delight. Aha! This was a fine punishment for Mother Go-Along! That would teach her to scold him! Oho!

He tipped up the can and sent down another lot of water – but this was too much for poor Mother Go-Along. When the fire said, 'Sizzle-sozzle,' again she ran out of the door squealing. 'Help! Help! There's a spell on my fire!' she cried.

Pippitty laughed so much that he fell right off the chimney and nearly slid down the roof. He decided to wait and see what would happen. Presently Mother Go-Along came back with Dame Quick-Eyes. Pippitty could hear them talking.

'I tell you there's a dreadful spell on my fire!' said Mother Go-Along. 'It keeps shouting "Sizzle-sozzle" at me, and sending out clouds of black smoke.'

'Dear, dear,' said Dame Quick-Eyes. 'Well, we must see what we can do about it!'

They went indoors. Pippitty put his ear to the chimney to hear what they said. He still had a little water left in his can. What fun to give Dame Quick-Eyes a fright too.

The fire was out. Dame Quick-Eyes told Mother Go-Along to make another. So in a few minutes sticks were burning merrily, and a nice fire roared up the chimney. The two dames sat down to see if the spell would work again.

They didn't have to wait long! Pippitty tipped up his can – splishy-sploshy-splishy-sploshy – down went the water, rushing through the chimney to the fire.

'Sizzle-sozzle-sizzle-sozzle!' shouted the fire and a cloud of smoke blew out! Dame Quick-Eyes had quick ears as well as quick eyes, and she had heard the splashing sound of the water – and she had seen too, the wetness that came around the hearth before the heat dried it up. *Some*one, yes, *some*one was pouring water down Mother Go-Along's chimney! Ho, ho! So that was it!

Dame Quick-Eyes whispered to Mother Go-Along.

'I'll catch the one who's doing this! Have you got a butterfly net or a fishing net anywhere about?'

'I've got an old fishing net in the cupboard,' whispered back Mother Go-Along. 'I'll get it. Whatever are you going to do?'

She fetched the net. Pippitty, who had his ear to the chimney, couldn't hear a word. He was longing to know if he had frightened Dame Quick-Eyes too!

Dame Quick-Eyes was busy – very busy! She had stolen to the door and opened it. She had rubbed a spell on the fishing net to make it bigger – and bigger – and bigger! It grew so long that it was higher than the roof! And then Dame Quick-Eyes looked up to the chimneys – and, very faintly indeed against the cloudy night sky, she spied someone sitting on the chimney! Aha!

She held up her long, long net – she held it just over the chimney – she brought it down on the chimney – smack! And she caught Pippitty!

What a surprise he got when that net came down on

him! He jumped so much that he almost fell down the chimney himself! He couldn't get out of the net, however much he struggled.

Dame Quick-Eyes twisted the net round, with Pippitty inside, and brought it down to the ground. She made the net smaller in a trice, put out her hand and grabbed Pippitty.

'So it's you, is it, you monkey!' she said. 'I might have guessed it!' She took the frightened pixie in to Mother Go-Along, who stared in surprise.

'Pippitty sat up on the roof and poured water down your chimney,' said Dame Quick-Eyes. 'That was what made the fire say "Sizzle-sozzle" and made the black smoke too. Do you want to scold him again, Mother Go-Along?'

'Oh, no, don't!' begged Pippitty.

'Scolding's no good for a naughty pixie like that,' said Mother Go-Along. 'I've tried it once – and see what happened. He just came and poured water down my chimney. No, Dame Quick-Eyes, I shall do something better than that. You said he was a monkey, so he shall be! When he's tired of being a real one, I'll turn him back into a pixie again and see if he can behave himself!'

She muttered three magic words over Pippitty – and in a trice he turned into a little brown monkey with big brown eyes and a long tail. What a shock for him that was!

He scurried away out of the cottage to hide himself. What *would* his friends say when they saw him? Oh, dear, oh, dear!

'He behaved like a monkey, and now that he is one he ought to be pleased,' said Dame Quick-Eyes.

But he wasn't! The funny thing is that now he *is* a monkey he doesn't behave like one – he behaves like a perfectly good pixie! I expect Mother Go-Along will change him back to his own shape soon – but if you happen to see a small monkey anywhere about with soft brown eyes, have a good look at him. It may be that rascal Pippitty!

The Enchanted Poker

The Enchanted Poker

'LOOK WHAT I've got!' said Scally to Wag. Wag looked.

'Ooooh – it's the enchanted magic poker, for tending the fire, isn't it? You'll get into trouble when he misses that, Scally!'

'He's away. His house is empty,' said Scally. 'So I slipped in to borrow it, just till he comes back, Wag. I can return it when he's home. But think how useful it will be to us!'

'How?' asked Wag.

'Well, who has to go and cut wood for the fire each day? We do. Who has to bring in the logs? We do.

Who has to put them on the fire and keep making it up? We do. Well – the poker will see to the fire now!' Scally grinned all over his face.

'Oh, I see. We make up the fire with wood – and then, whenever it burns down, we stick the poker into it, say a magic word, and it makes the fire burn again, without any fresh wood!' said Wag. 'Yes – a very good idea – no more wood cutting for us – just the magic poker at work. Good!'

The two imps lived with their old Aunt Mutter. She was cross and strict and didn't stand any nonsense at all. She worked them very hard – but now they could skip off to play instead of cutting wood. Hurrah!

'Put it by the fireplace,' said Wag. 'It's so like Aunt Mutter's poker that she'll never notice the difference.'

Scally stood the magic poker by the fireplace and hid the other poker in a cupboard. 'The fire's going down,' said Wag. 'Let's see how this poker does its work. What's the magic word, Scally?'

Scally whispered it to him. The poker heard it and

stirred. It hopped to the fire, gave it a violent poke and hopped back again to its place. The fire blazed up and crackled merrily!

'Goodness – it's better than I thought!' said Scally. 'We just say the word – and the poker does the trick. Wonderful!'

'Shh! Here's Aunt Mutter,' said Wag, as his plump, sharp-eyed aunt came in. She looked at the fire.

'Ah – burning up well – and a good thing for you it is! There's more wood needed, so go and cut it. I'm going to take a snooze in my chair.'

The two imps ran out, chuckling. Cut wood? Not they! Aunt Mutter sat herself down and took up her knitting. The fire died down a little, and the poker knew it ought to poke it. It stirred a little and Aunt Mutter looked up.

'What's that noise? Just the fire, I suppose. Dear me, I'm sleepy. I think I'll take a nap.'

She put down her knitting and shut her eyes. She snored a little.

Soon the fire died down a little more, and the poker got quite uneasy. It knew it ought to poke the fire. But it couldn't unless somebody said the magic word. Where were those imps who knew the word?

The poker suddenly left its place by the fire and hopped on its one leg round the kitchen. Hop-hop-hoppitty-hop! It made quite a noise on the stone floor. Aunt Mutter woke up with a jump.

'Now who's that? Is it you, Scally and Wag, hopping about? Just keep still or I'll give you something to make you hop still more!'

The poker hid behind the dresser, waiting till Aunt Mutter fell asleep again. Then out it came and hopped to the window. It looked out. Where were Scally and Wag?

They didn't come and the fire almost went out. The poker got very worried indeed. Perhaps Aunt Mutter knew the magic word? It hopped cautiously over to her and poked her in the leg.

She woke up at once and rubbed her leg. 'What was

that? Was it you, Puss, rubbing against me? Leave me alone, do!'

She shut her eyes again, and slept. The poker gave her a jab on the other leg and Aunt Mutter sat up with a yell.

'What's happening? Stop it! Jabbing me like this!' She looked all round but she couldn't see the poker, which was hiding under an armchair. The cat wasn't there either. Aunt Mutter began to feel very puzzled.

Bang, bang! That was somebody knocking at the door. 'Come in!' called Aunt Mutter.

In came old Mr Shuffle, beaming all over his face. 'Just come to say how-do-you-do,' he said.

'Ah, that's nice of you. Sit down in the armchair there,' said Aunt Mutter. 'I'll put the kettle on for a cup of tea. Dear, dear – the fire's gone down low. Where's the poker?'

The poker wasn't there, of course. It was under the armchair, and Mr Shuffle was at that very moment sitting down in the chair, making it creak loudly.

Aunt Mutter was cross. No poker – no wood to put on the fire – and no Scally and Wag to bring some in either. Dear, dear – she'd never get the kettle to boil on a fire like that.

She opened a cupboard door – and there was her poker – the one that Scally and Wag had hidden when they had brought in the magic one. Aunt Mutter was surprised to see it there. She took it and poked up the fire briskly. Then she put some coal on as there was no wood.

The poker under the chair tried to get out when it saw Aunt Mutter using another poker. Mr Shuffle heard it and looked down. 'I think your cat must be under here,' he said. 'I can feel her struggling to get out.'

'Now don't you get up,' said Aunt Mutter. 'Puss can easily get out if she wants to. She shouldn't get under chairs. I think she must have been under mine this afternoon – jabbing her claws into my leg!'

The poker grew desperate. It gave Mr Shuffle

a hard poke, and Mr Shuffle almost jumped out of his skin.

'Your cat's trying to bite me or something,' he said. 'Oooh – there it goes again – why, it's jabbing me.'

'Bless us all!' said Aunt Mutter, alarmed. 'Get up, Mr Shuffle, before she does you any damage. Move your chair.'

So Mr Shuffle got up and moved his chair. The magic poker hopped out at once and went to Aunt Mutter, who stared in alarm. 'What's this? A poker – a hopping poker? Get away, you tiresome thing!'

The poker hopped all round her, longing for her to say the magic word that would make it poke the fire so that it would burn brightly. She was frightened and poured water over it from the kettle. Then it hopped to Mr Shuffle, and he went and hid himself in a cupboard. He simply couldn't bear pokers that acted like that.

Then in came Scally and Wag, thinking that it must be teatime. The poker jigged over to them, and they stared in horror. Why – Aunt Mutter's own poker now stood by the fireplace, and the magic one was hopping about for everyone to see. What would Aunt Mutter say if they told her they had taken it from the enchanter's empty house? She would be very, very angry.

'Scally! Wag! Where did this poker come from?' cried their aunt.

'I don't know anything about it,' said Scally most untruthfully. 'It must have escaped from some witch or some wizard, Aunt. I'll chase it outdoors.'

But it was the poker who chased Scally, and jabbed at him. In the end, Wag took a stick and hit at the poker. It fell over, and Scally kicked it out of the kitchen. He slammed the door. Wag looked out of the window.

'It's hopping away,' he said. He whispered in Scally's ear. 'It's gone back to the enchanter's house, I expect.'

There was no further sign of the poker, and

everyone sat down to tea. Scally and Wag were rather scared afterwards when their aunt sent them out to get in more wood. Suppose that poker was lying in wait for them?

But it wasn't. They brought in some wood, and hoped that Aunt Mutter wouldn't notice that there was now very little in the woodshed. Mr Shuffle said good evening and went. The two imps wondered whether the poker would see him and chase him. But no doubt it was standing safely in its own fireplace by now.

Now, when they were in bed that night, Wag woke up with a jump. He sat up and listened. Tap-tap-tappitty-tap! Tap-tap-tappitty-tap! He could hear a tapping noise quite distinctly in the yard outside. Oh, dear – could it be the poker back again? Wag woke Scally and the two lay and listened to the tappitty noise outside.

Their bedroom was on the ground floor, and very soon there came a tapping noise at the window.

Tap-tap-tappy-tappy-tap!

'It's that poker back again!' whispered Wag. 'It will break the window! We'd better let it in and stand it by the fireplace. Bother it!'

So Wag opened the window, and in hopped the poker. It was shivering. It had been all the way back to the enchanter's house but it couldn't find any place to get in. So it had come back to stand by Aunt Mutter's warm fire.

But there was no fire. It had gone right out. The poker had a look at it and hopped all the way back from the kitchen to the imps' bedroom.

'It's back again,' said Scally in despair. It hopped up on to the bed, slithered between the warm blankets and lay there, stiff and straight.

'We can't have it in bed with us!' said Wag and kicked it out. But it was back again in a second and gave him such a jab that he cried out.

It was a dreadful night for the imps. Every time they moved the poker jabbed them – and in the early morning it pushed and poked them till they had to get out of bed and dress. It wanted them to make the fire and light it, so that it could go and stand in the warmth, where it usually stood. Poor Scally and Wag, they had never been up so early in their lives before!

Aunt Mutter saw the poker standing quietly beside her own poker at the side of the fireplace. She gaped in surprise. 'You don't mean to say it's back again!' she said. 'Wag and Scally, just tell me truthfully – where did that poker come from?'

Scally began to cry. He told his aunt all about the magic poker, and she was full of horror.

'What! It belongs to the enchanter – and you've been using its magic? What do you suppose he will say when he hears? Why, he might quite well change you both into pokers yourselves, and then what would you do?'

The poker thought this was very funny and shook with laughter, though it didn't make a sound. Scally and Wag glared at it. Horrid thing – jabbing them –

and now laughing. They couldn't even use it now, for they didn't dare to say the magic word.

'Oh, Aunt Mutter – what shall we do? The enchanter is away, so we can't give him back the poker,' wept Wag. 'And we can't put up with it here.'

'Oh, yes, we can,' said Aunt Mutter. 'Hey, poker! You can stay here till your master comes back, and we won't use your magic at all – but let me tell you this – if you want to chase these two bad imps and make them do their work well, I'd be glad. You do that!'

The poker shook with laughter again, and hopped out from the fireplace at once. It chased Scally to the sink to make him begin the washing up, and it chased Wag outside to fetch some wood. Aha! It was going to have a very fine time.

Aunt Mutter is very pleased with it. In fact, she is thinking of buying it from the enchanter when he returns. That would be a shock for Scally and Wag!

The Kite with a Tail

The Kite with a Tail

'GOT YOU!' said a loud voice, and somebody pounced on Pippi the pixie.

'Oooh! Let me go!' yelled Pippi. 'Help, help, where are you, Tricky? Help!'

'Tricky ran off when he saw me coming,' said Sniff the goblin, holding Pippi tightly. 'Oho! So I've got you at last, you mischievous little pixie. Always playing tricks on me and making me cross. Well, now I've caught you, and I shall take you home and keep you prisoner. I shall put a spell all round my house so that you can't possibly get away.'

Pippi the pixie was dragged off by the goblin,

who was twice as big as Pippi, and had a beard that almost reached the ground.

Tricky, Pippi's brother, watched from behind a tree. He was very scared. Sniff was a powerful goblin, and now he would make Pippi his servant, and never, never let him go. Oh, why had he and Pippi played tricks on him, booing at him from behind trees, and calling rude names after him?

'It's too late to think that now,' said Tricky to himself. 'What I've got to do is to try and find some way of rescuing Pippi.'

But that wasn't at all easy. Sniff the goblin grew a high wall all round his little house and garden, so that nobody could possibly get in unless he let them in himself. There was a spell in the wall, and anyone who tried to climb it fell off with a bump long before he reached the top. Nothing could be thrown over the wall, because Sniff had put another spell at the top, and whenever anything was thrown up, it just came flying back.

Tricky ran everywhere to try and get help for Pippi. But nobody could help him, because they knew how powerful Sniff's spells were, and they didn't know how to take the magic away from the wall.

Then one day Tricky met Cinders, his grandmother's black cat. She had green eyes and had belonged to a witch. She was an old cat now, and only wanted to laze by the fire, so the witch had sold her, because she was no more use for helping to make spells.

'Hallo, Tricky,' mewed Cinders. 'How's Pippi?'

'Oh, didn't you know? He was caught by Sniff the goblin, and he's being kept a prisoner behind the high walls,' said Tricky. 'I simply don't know how to rescue him.'

'Sniff the goblin? Now – let me see,' said Cinders, and her long whiskers twitched to and fro. 'Yes, I remember now. He has a cat, as black as I am, with eyes as green as cucumbers. What's his name now – oh, yes, Pad-About. Well, Pad-About is my great-grandson – or is it my great-great? I forget.'

Tricky waited patiently while the old black cat washed her back and went on talking.

'Now, you tell Pippi to say "Creamy buns" to Pad-About, and he'll know it's a message from me, and he'll help Pippi,' said Cinders, beginning to lick her front thoroughly.

'"Creamy buns!" What a funny message to send!' said Tricky.

'It isn't really. I once had Pad-About to stay with me, when I belonged to Witch Red-Cloak,' said Cinders, 'and he so far forgot himself as to eat a plate of creamy buns in the witch's larder. Well, they had a very strong spell in them, and when I next saw Pad-About his furry head had turned into a cream bun. So I had to go and explain matters to the witch and beg for a spell to change him back.'

'Good gracious! What a dreadful thing to happen to anyone,' said Tricky, making up his mind never to eat cream buns in a witch's house.

'Yes, it was. I felt so ashamed,' said Cinders.

'Such a thing had never happened in my family before. Pad-About was very, very grateful for my help. And whenever I want to send him a message and make sure that he knows it's from me, I say "Creamy buns". Pippi's only got to say that to him, and Pad-About will at once help him for my sake.'

'Thank you very, very much,' said Tricky and went off happily. But he hadn't gone very far before he began to think how dreadfully difficult it was going to be to get the message through to Pippi. How could he? He couldn't climb over the wall. He couldn't throw anything over because it just came back. He couldn't shout, or Sniff would know he was there and take him prisoner too. Then how was he to get the message to Pippi?

I'll send him a letter, thought Tricky at last. But no, that wouldn't do, because Sniff would be sure to read it. Tricky went on home, sighing as he tried to think of some good plan.

Then someone called to him. It was little Hickory

in the field beyond. 'Hi, Tricky! Look at my lovely kite!'

Tricky looked. The kite flew up in the air and then, alas, dipped right down to the ground and lay still.

'It keeps doing that,' shouted Hickory sadly. 'It just won't fly properly.'

'You want a tail for it,' said Tricky. 'Come to my house and I'll make one for your kite.'

So back they went to the house. Tricky cut up some paper, and showed Hickory how to fold it and tie each piece to a long string, to make the tail.

'Wait,' said Hickory, and he took a pencil out of his pocket. 'I want to write a message on this tail – so that if my kite flies away from me and somebody else finds it, they will read my name and address on the tail, and bring it back to me.'

So Hickory wrote on each piece of paper before he tied it to the tail. He put his name on the first bit – 'Hickory'. He put half his address on the second bit – 'Hollyhock Cottage'. The other half went on the third bit – 'Cherry Town'. Then he put a word on each of the other bits that made the tail, so that his message read, 'Please return me my kite.'

'There! Aren't I clever?' he said, as he tied on the last piece.

Tricky stared at him, a wonderful idea coming into his mind. 'Yes – you're *very* clever, Hickory. Cleverer than you think!'

And when Hickory had gone out happily to fly his kite with its new long tail, Tricky began to make a very fine plan of his own.

'I'll get a kite – and I'll make it a tail of bits of paper tied to a string, like Hickory's – and I'll put one word on each bit of paper, so that if only I can fly it over the wall into Sniff's garden, Pippi will find it, and perhaps read the message!' Tricky was so thrilled with his plan that he danced all round the kitchen in joy.

He remembered that Pippi had a kite. That was fine! Pippi would know it, and guess there was some trick about its falling into Sniff's garden. Tricky thought he had better write a cheeky message on the kite's face, so that Sniff would see it and think Tricky had sent the kite just to be rude to him.

So he set to work. He got out the kite, which was a big one with a smiling face painted on it. He made it a fine new tail of bits of paper. There were ten pieces, and Tricky wrote his message twice, one word on each piece of paper. This is the message he wrote:

'Say Creamy Buns to Pad-About. Say Creamy Buns to Pad-About.'

Tricky grinned. What a silly message it seemed. Never mind, it would work all right if only Pippi read it and acted on it.

He went out into the windy March afternoon. How the wind blew! Just the day for flying kites.

He went to the field that lay outside Sniff's house. Up went the kite into the air. Besides the message on the bits of paper in the tail there was another message on the face of the kite itself. It really sounded very rude.

'Tell Sniff to put himself in his dustbin!'

Tricky grinned when he thought of that message. He felt sure that Sniff would be so angry when he saw it that he wouldn't even think of looking at the papers in the tail.

The kite flew high in the air, bearing its two messages. It flew right above Sniff's walled-in garden. Then Tricky jerked hard at the string, and the kite dipped down in surprise. Tricky let the string go loose – and the kite dipped in circles right down to Sniff's garden. It fell on the grass, and lay there, flapping a little in the wind.

Sniff saw it at once. 'Ho! So somebody has sent a kite into my garden!' he stormed. 'Go and get it, and bring it here, Pippi.'

Pippi went to get it. He felt very frightened when he saw that it was his own kite, and that Tricky had scribbled such a rude message on it.

'Tell Sniff to put himself in the dustbin!' Oh, dear, oh, dear! What in the world would Sniff say?

Sniff said a lot. He shouted and yelled. Then he flung the kite on the floor and jumped on it till it was completely spoilt.

'If your brother thinks tricks of this sort are going to make me any kinder to you he can think again,' roared Sniff. 'Stupid, silly, ridiculous fellow!'

Pippi was very upset. He, too, thought it was very, very silly of Tricky. He sat in a corner and moped.

Surely Tricky couldn't be so very stupid? Surely he must have sent the kite for something else besides a piece of mischief?

He sat and stared at where the kite lay on the floor, its tail forlornly dragging behind it. And quite suddenly he saw part of a word written on one of the bits of paper that made the tail. His heart began to beat very quickly indeed.

There must be another message on the tail – but a message for me this time! thought Pippi in excitement. *Tricky sent the rude message to attract Sniff's attention – but the other hidden message is for me. Oh, how can I manage to read it?*

He soon had his chance, because Sniff told him to take the kite and burn it on the kitchen fire. Pippi gathered it up and went into the kitchen, where Pad-About, Sniff's big black cat, was sitting dreaming by the fire.

'Move yourself,' said Pippi, but Pad-About wouldn't. He was not a good-tempered cat, and had already scratched Pippi three times.

Pippi crammed the kite itself into the fire. He put all the tail into his pocket, and waited for Sniff to go out. As soon as the goblin had slammed the front door, Pippi took out the kite's tail, and with trembling fingers undid the bits of paper. He read the words on them.

'Say Creamy Buns to Pad-About. Say Creamy Buns to Pad-About.' Pippi stared at the extraordinary words. He could not make head or tail of them. He looked at them till he felt he could never forget them, and then he threw all the bits of paper into the fire.

He looked at Pad-About. Pad-About stared back rudely, and then yawned widely.

'Creamy buns,' said Pippi suddenly. 'CREAMY BUNS!'

Pad-About stopped yawning at once. He stared at Pippi as if he couldn't believe his eyes.

'I said – "CREAMY BUNS!"' said Pippi. 'Go on – it's a message for you. What about it?'

'It's a message from my great-great-grandmother, the black cat called Cinders, who used to belong to a powerful witch,' said Pad-About, in a curious purring voice. 'Only friends of hers know those words – creamy buns. If you are a friend of hers, I must help you. I think you are a rude little pixie, but if my great-great-grandmother wishes it, I must be a friend to you.'

'Good old creamy buns,' said Pippi. 'Well, Pad-About, I don't much like you either – you use your claws too much. But if you're going to help me, I'll change my mind about you. Now – how can you help me? Can you get me out of here?'

'Of course,' said Pad-About. 'See that bottle up there – full of yellow stuff? That's to make you small. Drink a teaspoonful, and you'll be small enough to go down that mouse hole. It leads under the house, down a tunnel and under the wall. It comes up the other side. You'll be free if you go down there – and I'll be glad to be rid of you.'

'Thanks!' said Pippi, and drank a teaspoonful of the yellow stuff from the bottle. Immediately he felt as if he was going down in a lift, and everything became simply enormous round him. He had become as small as a mouse! He looked at Pad-About, who now seemed to him to be as large as an elephant, and looked exactly like a giant black tiger!

Pippi decided to be very, very polite to him. 'Thank you very much, Pad-About,' he said. 'If ever I can get a few creamy buns for you, I'll be delighted.'

But that wasn't at all the right thing to say, and Pad-About put out a paw full of very sharp claws at once. Pippi shot down the mouse hole in fright, and ran all the way till he came out under the wall, and found himself standing at the outlet of the hole in the field beyond. He had bumped into two or three startled mice, but that was all.

Still very small indeed, he tore across the field and after a long time he arrived at his own cottage. He hammered at the door, but couldn't make much noise with his tiny fists. Still Tricky heard him and opened the door. He couldn't see anyone at first, because Pippi wasn't even as tall as his shoe.

'It's me, Pippi!' cried Pippi, in a voice as high and squeaky as a mouse's. Tricky couldn't believe his eyes. He picked Pippi up and put him on the table.

'You've gone small. Where's my Bigger Spell? Oh, here it is. Stay still, Pippi, and let me blow it on you.'

It wasn't long before Pippi was his own size again, and the two gave one another a bear-like hug.

'You *were* clever to send that message on the kite's

tail!' cried Pippi. 'It did the trick! Pad-About just *had* to help me – and here I am!'

'What a sell for old Sniff!' said Tricky. 'But all the same, Pippi, let's not play any more tricks on him. It's dangerous.'

So they didn't – but I expect you know what they yell at poor old Pad-About whenever they see him? Yes – CREAMY BUNS!

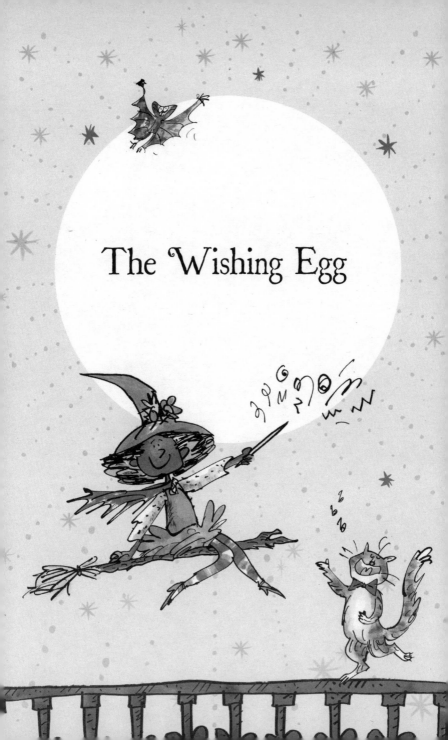

The Wishing Egg

The Wishing Egg

ONE DAY Dame Slippers was given a curious spell. It was a tiny pea, hard and dry – but it wasn't brown or green – it was bright blue.

'Feed it to one of your hens, Dame Slippers,' said her friend, Mother Very-Old. 'And it will lay a wishing egg. It will be very useful to you, because once a week you can turn the egg over and over in your hands till it's warm – and then you can wish a wish!'

Well, Dame Slippers was very pleased about that. She could do with a few wishes! She was a good old woman and would never wish a wrong wish. Now – which hen should she give the magic pea to?

I'll give it to Speckled Feathers! she thought. *She always lays a nice big egg, so perhaps the wishes will be all the better for that.*

She went out and threw the little blue pea on the ground in front of Speckled Feathers. The hen snapped it up at once. Good. Now, her very next egg would be a wishing egg! Dame Slippers shut Speckled Feathers up in a coop by herself that night, so that she would know she had the right egg, if the hen laid one.

But that night little Sneaky came along to see what he could find. He had been to Old Man Shuffle and had taken a lettuce from his garden. He had been to Mrs Look-About, and had pulled a couple of carrots, and he had taken an apple off Jim-Jim's tree. Now he was sneaking round Dame Slippers's back gate.

I'll look for an egg, he thought. *She keeps hens. I could do with one for my breakfast.*

He saw a coop standing by itself. Was a hen there? Yes – he could dimly see the gleam of Speckled Feathers sitting on the perch there. He opened the door and groped in the little nesting box.

Good, there was an egg! He slipped it into his pocket, shut the door and crept away home. But on the way he met Mother Hurry, rushing along to her daughter's. She stopped Sneaky.

'Sneaky – my daughter is ill. I am going to give her an egg beaten up in milk, but the shops are shut and I can't buy one. Can you let me have one?'

'Yes, certainly!' said Sneaky, feeling in his pocket. 'One shilling, Dame Hurry.'

'What a wicked price!' said Dame Hurry, and paid out a shilling. 'I'd never pay it if I wasn't in such a hurry to get to my daughter!'

She hurried off – but when she came to her daughter's cottage, she found that the doctor had said she must not have eggs at all. So she had spent a whole shilling for nothing!

Dame Hurry was cross, but when the next morning came and her daughter was much better, she felt happy.

'Well, I don't want an egg for *my* breakfast,' she said, 'so I'll just pop in and leave it for Mrs Honey's little girl. She's having a birthday today, so it can go into her cake and make it really good.'

She left the egg with Tippy the little girl – but when she gave it to her mother, Mrs Honey laughed. 'Dear me – I made your cake last week!' she said. 'And it had *six* eggs in it! Run across to Old Man Heyho, dear, and give it to him. He dearly loves an egg for tea.'

So the little girl ran across to Old Man Heyho. He wasn't there, so she handed it to his servant to give to him. 'He's away, but he's coming back today,' said the maid. 'I'll cook it for his tea.'

But Old Man Heyho sent word to say that he wasn't coming home till the next week, after all – so his maid wondered what to do with the egg.

I'll give it to Mr High-Hat, Old Man Heyho's friend, she thought. *That's the best thing to do!*

So she wrapped it up, and put a little note with it.

'For Mr High-Hat with best wishes from Old Man Heyho.' There wasn't anyone in Mr High-Hat's house, so she left the egg in the middle of the table with the note.

'Dear, dear!' said Mr High-Hat, when he came in from his shopping and found it. 'An egg! Old Man Heyho must have forgotten that I have at least twenty hens myself! Now what shall I do with it?'

Well, at that very moment, who should come knocking at his door but Dame Slippers. 'Come in!' called Mr High-Hat. 'Oh, it's you, Dame Slippers. Do you want an egg? Someone has just left me one and I don't want it.'

'Well, I keep hens, but not an egg did they give me this morning,' said Dame Slippers, and she picked up the one on Mr High-Hat's table and turned it over and over in her hands. 'I'd be glad of this. I was hoping I'd have an egg from Speckled Feathers, my best hen – a wishing egg, Mr High-Hat. I heard her cackle in the night to tell me she had laid one – but a thief must have come and taken it.'

'Dear, dear – what a waste of a wishing egg!' said Mr High-Hat. 'It will probably be eaten, and the eater will never know it was a wishing egg!'

'Yes – it's a pity,' said Dame Slippers. 'I was going to wish all kinds of good wishes – a new pair of shoes for Mother Barefoot; a shawl for Dame Cold; a new barrow for Mr Workalot; dear me, how I *wish* I knew who the mean little thief was who stole that wishing egg! I just *wish* he was standing here before me!'

Well, of course, she was holding the wishing egg in her hand! It had travelled quite a way since it had left the nesting box – but it had got right back to her at last! And her wish came true.

Sneaky was at that very minute getting off a bus near his home. The moment that Dame Slippers wished her wish he felt himself whisked round – and his feet began running at top speed towards Mr High-Hat's cottage! How astonished he was!

'What's happening! Why can't I stop myself?

There's a spell on me! Oh my, oh my!'

He didn't stop till he was in High-Hat's Cottage, standing in front of Dame Slippers, out of breath. She stared at him in surprise – then she looked at the egg in her hand.

'Why – can *this* be the wishing egg? What an extraordinary thing! Sneaky, answer me truthfully – was it you who stole an egg from Speckled Feathers's nesting box last night?'

'Yes, it was! Oh, forgive me!' cried Sneaky, who was most alarmed at what had just happened to him.

'Well, well – I've got my wishing egg after all, Mr High-Hat!' said Dame Slippers, pleased. 'And all because of you. When I wish a wish next week, I'll wish for a fine new hat for you, the biggest you've got!'

And off she went, holding the wishing egg carefully in her hand.

The Train that Wouldn't Stop

The Train that Wouldn't Stop

IN THE nursery of the Princess Marigold was a toy train.

It was a very fine one indeed. It was made of wood, painted all colours. It didn't run on lines; it trundled wherever it liked, round and round the nursery.

It was rather a magic train. In the cab of the red engine was a little knob. When Princess Marigold pressed the knob, the train began to run along, pulling the carriages behind in a long string. And it would go on running until the princess said the word 'Hattikattikooli'.

Then the train would stop suddenly and stand

absolutely still until the knob in the engine's cab was once again pressed.

Marigold had great fun with the train. She set all her dolls and toys in it, pressed the knob, and off they went, trundling up and down. Sometimes she opened the door of her nursery and the train would rattle all down the passage and back, startling the king very much if he met it suddenly round a corner.

Now there were two small pixies who lived just outside the palace walls in a pansy bed. They were Higgle and Tops, and *how* they loved that little toy train. One day they had climbed up the ivy, right up the wall, and in at the princess's window to see the train running.

They sat hidden behind a big doll on the windowsill, watching for the train to start.

Marigold put the sailor doll into the cab of the engine to drive it. She put all the Noah's ark animals into two of the carriages, her doll and teddy bear in the next one, and all the skittles in the rest. Higgle and Tops nearly fell off the windowsill trying to see what she did to start up the engine.

'She pressed a little knob!' whispered Higgle into Tops's ear, making him jump. 'She did! That's how you start it!'

'I know. I saw,' said Tops. 'Oh, Higgle, if only the princess would go out of the room for a bit we could have a ride in that train!'

And would you believe it, somebody called Marigold at that moment, and she ran out of the room, closing the door behind her in case the train got out.

In a minute Higgle and Tops were down on the floor, running across to the moving train. Higgle got hold of the sailor doll. 'Get out!' he cried. 'You can't drive for toffee! Let *me* drive!'

The sailor doll pushed Higgle away. The doll began to shout. The bear tried to get out of his carriage to go to the sailor doll's help.

When Tops began to pull at the sailor doll too, he just had to fall off the engine. Then Higgle and

Tops leapt into the cab and began to drive. Oh, how lovely!

They drove round and round the nursery at such a tremendous speed that three of the skittles fell out, and the kangaroo in one of the front carriages was frightened and jumped out in a hurry.

'Stop!' called the doll. 'You'll smash us all up! Stop, I tell you!'

But Higgle and Tops had never driven a train before in their lives and they weren't going to stop! No, they went faster and faster and faster. And when Marigold came back she was horrified to see her little train tearing by like a mad thing with all the toys hanging on for dear life and shouting in fright.

'Hattikattikooli!' she cried, and the train stopped so suddenly that everyone was shot into the air, and fell in a heap on the hearth rug. The pixies shot out too, and ran behind the doll's house to hide. They were trembling with excitement.

'Sailor doll!' said Marigold sternly, looking round

for the indignant sailor doll. 'Is *that* how you drive the train when I am out of the room? For shame!'

Behind the doll's house was a little mouse hole. Higgle nudged Tops. 'Look! A mouse hole! We'd better get down it before the toys come after us. They'll be dreadfully angry.'

So down the mouse hole they both crept. It was very small, and they had to crawl on their tummies – but, goodness me, it led right to the garden! That *was* a bit of luck for Higgle and Tops.

When the toys came to look for them behind the doll's house, meaning to give them punishment for their naughtiness, they were not there. 'Just wait!' the sailor doll shouted down the mouse hole. 'Just wait, you two! Next time you come we'll give you such a scolding!'

Higgle and Tops talked and talked about the train. How lovely it was to drive! If only it was theirs! What long journeys they could go on – what adventures they could have!

'Let's borrow it,' said Higgle at last. 'Tops, we simply *must* drive it again. Let's go tonight and get it. We can creep up the mouse hole. We know how to start it. Do let's.'

'I'd love to,' said Tops at once. 'Oh, Higgle! Think of driving that train up and down hill, all across the countryside and everywhere!'

Well, that night the two of them went up the mouse hole again, and into the nursery. The train was standing quietly in the corner. The toys were all at the other end, dancing to the musical box. The sailor doll was turning the handle, and nobody was looking round at all.

'Now's our chance!' whispered Higgle, and the two pixies made a rush for the train. They got into the cab, pressed the knob – and off they went!

The toys stopped dancing in fright and surprise. The train rushed by them and out of the open nursery door. Gracious! Where could it be going?

'It's those pixies. They've taken our train! How

dare they!' cried the doll in a rage. But there was nothing to be done about it. The train was gone.

It flew down the passage, bumped down a hundred stairs, ran to the garden door – and out it went into the garden!

'Here we go!' yelled Higgle in delight. 'Where to? We don't know and we don't care! Go on, train, go on, faster, faster, faster!'

All that night the train sped ever fields and hills, through valleys and towns. When the dawn came, it turned to go back. Higgle and Tops had no idea at all where they were. They were just enjoying going faster and faster. The train hurried back over the hills and fields.

'I say – look!' said Higgle suddenly. Tops looked – and there, not very far in front of them, were two red goblins, fighting hard. The pixies were very frightened indeed of goblins.

'Stop the train,' said Higgle. 'We don't want the goblins to see it. They'll catch it for their own.'

'I can't remember the word to stop it,' said Tops.
'You say it, Higgle.'

But Higgle couldn't remember it either! Oh, dear!
Now they would never be able to stop the train! It flew
on towards the fighting, yelling goblins, and knocked
them both flat on their backs. The pixies just had time
to see an open sack filled with shining jewels as they
passed. Then the train shot into a cave, bumped against
the wall, buried itself in earth and stopped with a
shudder and a sigh. Its wheels went round still, but
the train didn't move. It couldn't!

Higgle and Tops were thrown out. They sat in the
dark cave trembling. They didn't dare to go out, in
case the goblins saw them.

Outside, the shouting still went on. 'You knocked
me flat!' cried one goblin to another. 'Take that – and
that – and that!'

The second goblin howled. 'Don't! Don't! I'll go
away now, really I will. You can have everything
yourself.'

There was the sound of running footsteps. One of the goblins had gone. 'Oho!' said the other. 'He's gone. Well, I shall hide all the goods and keep guard over them. He may come back. I don't trust him!'

Higgle and Tops were sitting in the middle of the cave, still trembling, when something hit them hard. They jumped. Goodness, it was a glittering necklace! The goblin must have thrown it into the cave.

'A necklace!' whispered Higgle. 'A real beauty! Where have they stolen it from?'

Blip! A ring hit Tops, and another hit Higgle on the shoulder. Then came a perfect shower of jewellery, falling all about the cave – thud, blip, crash! It soon looked like a treasure cave, and Higgle and Tops didn't know where to go to avoid being hit as the goblin threw everything into the cave to hide it.

'My word!' whispered Tops at last. 'I believe all this belongs to the queen herself, Princess Marigold's mother. Imagine it, Higgle! Those goblins must have broken in and stolen all this last night.'

'Well – how are we to get it back to the palace?' asked Higgle. 'Look outside there – the goblin is sitting at the entrance to this cave, guarding his treasure. We'll never get past him carrying all this. He'd catch us at once.'

'We can't stay here for ever though,' said Tops. 'It's cold and uncomfortable – and I'm getting hungry. Think of something, Higgle. Use your brains.'

'Use yours!' said Higgle. So they sat and thought and the only noise in the cave was the sound of the train wheels still going round and round, though the train could not move.

'*I* know!' said Higgle at last. 'Let's pull the train out of the earth it's buried in, and go out in that. We can pile the jewels in the carriages.'

'And they'll all be jerked out!' said Tops.

'I'll tell you what we'll do!' said Higgle, getting excited. 'We'll wind all the necklaces and bracelets and chains round the wheels. They'll keep on then. And we'll drop the rings down the engine funnel.

They'll stay there all right. Come on, Tops!'

They set to work. They wound the shining necklaces and bracelets and chains round and round the wheels. Then they dropped all the rings down the funnel. The train looked very jolly indeed when they had finished with it.

'I guess a train was never dressed up like this before!' said Higgle, pleased. 'Now come on, Tops – help me to pull it out of this earth. Steady on! Jump in as soon as we've got it free, because it will shoot out of the cave at top speed. It's still going, you know! We haven't thought of the word to stop the wheels turning yet!'

At last they got the engine out of the earth, and it stood upright. The wheels turned swiftly. Higgle and Tops jumped into the cab just as the train began to move. It went twice round the cave and then shot out of the entrance full speed ahead, its wheels glittering and gleaming in the morning sun.

How it shone with all its jewels! The goblin

stared open-mouthed at this sudden, extraordinary appearance of what looked to him like a glittering snake.

The train rushed over his legs and made him yell. Before he could grab it, it disappeared, shining brilliantly. The pixies laughed. 'That was a fine idea of ours! We've escaped with all the jewels without being caught!'

The train didn't need to be told to go to the palace. It longed to be home! It shot off and soon came to the garden. It couldn't find any door open and raced up and down the paths like a mad thing. The king and queen saw it and stared in amazement as it ran by them.

'What is it? It's all shining and glittering,' said the king. 'It's as bright as those lovely jewels of yours that were stolen during the night, my love!'

Princess Marigold appeared. 'Mother! Did you know my magic train was stolen? It's gone!'

At that moment the train shot back again up the path, shining brilliantly, with the jewels round all its wheels. Marigold gave a squeal.

'Hattikattikooli! Hattikattikooli!'

Thankfully the train stopped just by her. She knelt down and looked at the wheels. 'Mother! It's brought back all your stolen jewels! Do look!'

Higgle and Tops got out of the engine and bowed. 'We brought them back to you,' said Higgle grandly. 'The two goblins stole them and hid them in a cave.'

'Dear me – how very clever and brave of you,' said the queen, pleased. 'You shall have a reward. I will give you a sackful of gold all for yourselves.'

'Thank you, madam!' said the pixies, beaming. Now they would be rich. 'We will take the train back to the nursery for you when you have taken all your jewels from the wheels and the funnel.'

They ran it back to the nursery, feeling very grand. The toys gazed at them in rage. Those pixies! They had taken the train all right!

'Good morning,' said Higgle, stepping out. 'We have an adventure to tell you. Listen!'

He told all that had happened. The toys listened. 'And,' said Higgle at the end, 'as a reward for bringing back the jewels, we are to get a sack of gold. Ha, a fine reward!'

'Have your reward if you like,' said the sailor doll. 'But let me tell you this – you're having a punishment too, for taking our train. Why, you might never have brought it back.'

Well, the pixies got their reward – but they also had their punishment too, which was quite as it should be. They were so pleased to be rich that they gave a fine party to all the toys, and everybody went for a ride round the nursery, driven by the pixies.

They forgot the word that stopped the train, of course – but that didn't matter because all the toys knew it. They yelled it out loudly. Let me see – *what* was it? Dear me, I've forgotten it too! Do *you* remember?

Acknowledgements

All efforts have been made to seek necessary permissions.

The stories in this publication first appeared in the following publications:

'The Story of Dilly and Daffo' first appeared in *The Teachers World*, No. 1145, 1926.

'Mr Very-Smart' first appeared in *The Teachers World*, No. 1472, 1931.

'The Pig with a Straight Tail' first appeared in *Sunny Stories for Little Folks*, No. 133, 1932.

'The Hey-Diddle Pie' first appeared in *Sunny Stories for Little Folks*, No. 117, 1931.

'Chuff the Chimney Sweep' first appeared in *Sunny Stories for Little Folks*, No. 120, 1931.

'The Enchanted Egg' first appeared in *Enid Blyton's Sunny Stories*, No. 403, 1947.

'A Pins and Needles Spell' first appeared in *Enid Blyton's Magazine*, No. 10, Vol. 6, 1958.

'The Magic Treacle Jug' first appeared in *Enid Blyton's Annual*, published by *Daily Express* in 1957.

'The Skippetty Shoes' first appeared in *Sunny Stories for Little Folks*, No. 233, 1936.

'Susie and Her Shadow' first appeared in *Enid Blyton's Sunny Stories*, No. 170, 1940.

'The Cat that Could Sing' first appeared in *Sunny Stories for Little Folks*, No. 213, 1935.

'The Conjuring Wizard' first appeared in *Sunny Stories for Little Folks*, No. 138, 1932.

'The Flyaway Broomstick' first appeared in *Sunny Stories for Little Folks*, No. 80, 1929.

'Humpty Dumpty' first appeared in *The Teachers World*, No. 1016, 1924.

'Meddle Does the Washing' first appeared in *Enid Blyton's Sunny Stories*, No. 421, 1948.

'Coltsfoot Magic' first appeared in *Enid Blyton's Sunny Stories*, No. 375, 1946.

'Five Times Five Are ...' first appeared in *You*, Issue 7, 1951.

'The Stolen Eggs' first appeared in *The Teachers World*, No. 1733, 1936.

'Four Little Wheels' first appeared in *Enid Blyton's Sunny Stories*, No. 342, 1944.

'The Magic Silver Thread' first appeared as 'The Biggest Giant in the World', in *Sunny Stories for Little Folks*, No. 123, 1931.

'Pippitty's Joke' first appeared in *Enid Blyton's Sunny Stories*, No. 69, 1938.

'The Enchanted Poker' first appeared as 'The Enchanter's Poker' in *Enid Blyton's Magazine*, No. 9, Vol. 1, 1953.

'The Kite with a Tail' first appeared in *Enid Blyton's Sunny Stories*, No. 427, 1948.

'The Wishing Egg' first appeared in *Enid Blyton's Magazine*, No. 16, Vol. 1, 1953.

'The Train that Wouldn't Stop' first appeared in *Enid Blyton's Sunny Stories*, No. 426, 1948.

Also available:

Enid Blyton

STORIES OF

MAGIC

AND

MISCHIEF

30 stories

A spellbinding selection of magical and
mischievous tales by the world's
best-loved storyteller!

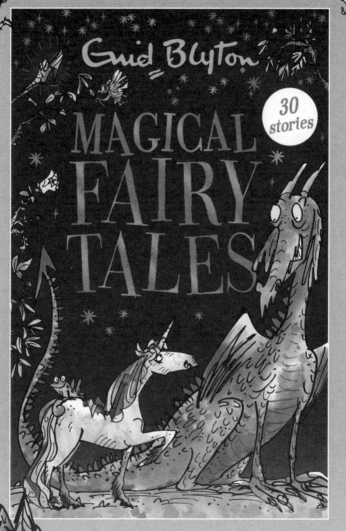

Enid Blyton

30 stories

MAGICAL FAIRY TALES

Delve into this enchanted collection of short stories, retold by the world's best-loved storyteller!

Enid Blyton

is one of the most popular children's authors of all time. Her books have sold over 500 million copies and have been translated into other languages more often than any other children's author.

Enid Blyton adored writing for children. She wrote over 700 books and about 2,000 short stories. *The Famous Five* books, now 80 years old, are her most popular. She is also the author of other favourites including *The Secret Seven*, *The Magic Faraway Tree* and *Malory Towers*.

Born in London in 1897, Enid lived much of her life in Buckinghamshire and loved dogs, gardening and the countryside. She was very knowledgeable about trees, flowers, birds and animals. Dorset – where some of the Famous Five's adventures are set – was a favourite place of hers too.

Enid Blyton's stories are read and loved by millions of children (and grown-ups) all over the world. Visit enidblyton.co.uk to discover more.

Illustration by
Laura Ellen Anderson.